I0523713

ZAPATA IS HERE!

A novel by Meridel LeSueur

This is a work of fiction. Names, characters, places, and incidents are either the product of the author's imagination or are used fictitiously.

Zapata Is Here! © 2025 by the estate of Meridel LeSueur.
Foreword © 2025 by David Tilsen.
The People Are a River by Irene Paull, reprinted with permission from Stage Left by The Alive and Trucking Theatre, Christopher Robin Printers, Minneapolis © 1973.
All Rights Reserved.

Published by Midwest Villages & Voices.
www.midwestvillages.com

No part of this work may be performed, recorded, or otherwise transmitted without written consent of the estate of Meridel LeSueur and the permission of the publisher. However, short portions may be cited for book reviews without obtaining consent.

First edition: 2025.

Copy editors:
David Tilsen, Lincoln Bergman, Barbara Tilsen, Gayla Ellis
Layout and design by Basil Shadid.
Front cover photo by Andrea Alonso, www.andreaalonso.mx.

Visit www.meridellesueur.org for more information about Meridel LeSueur.
ISBN: 978-0-935697-16-2

ZAPATA IS HERE!

A novel by Meridel LeSueur

Midwest Villages & Voices
2025

Foreword

My most vivid memory from my childhood is a family trip to Mexico. My parents piled three adults—the two of them and my grandmother Meridel LeSueur—and six children into a station wagon pulling a trailer and left from Minneapolis, Minnesota for what became a three-month trip. We took about a week of driving to end up in a Mexican town called San Luis Potosi. There we stayed for at least two weeks. Every day we would drop my grandmother off at a home, library, market or town square. She would haul her materials which included a "portable" tape recorder, which was reel-to-reel, weighed over 30 pounds, and took a dozen C cell batteries, if electricity could not be found.

As I think about it now, it seems amazing to me. I imagine that she went up to strangers and in her non-native language asked elders if they knew Zapata or if they had stories that were passed down, or knew of people who did. What courage and confidence! And people spoke to her, presumably trusted her. That was Meridel, no guile, just intelligence, integrity, empathy and understanding.

She explained to me that the reason for this trip was to

do research into a leader of the Mexican revolution named Emiliano Zapata. She sought out people who knew him, saw him speak, or who had heard stories about him from elders they had known. After we left San Luis Potosí, we went to other smaller towns in Mexico, where she continued to talk to people, going to local markets and libraries, while we children explored, went to the sea or played in parks. She remarked on what a great resource local librarians were. She received a lot of leads and information from them. We had a lot of time in the car where Meridel would tell us about Zapata, what life was like back then and how the people struggled to survive and free themselves from colonialism. I soaked it all up.

Sixty years later, as I was going through records after my parents died, I came across a treasure: the unpublished manuscript of a book by Meridel simply entitled *Zapata*. This was the book she was researching during our family trip. We decided to rename it *Zapata Is Here!*—a line from the book itself: The whole village was running, crying, "It's Zapata! Zapata is here!" The new title reflects the real heart of the book. This is not a biography of Zapata, but a story of how his spirit transormed the people, the movement, and their collective fight for land and freedom.

During the 1950s and 1960s, Meridel was not able to sell her writings—poetry, prose, journalism and Midwest radical history that had supported her for the previous thirty years. She turned to writing young adult books about historical figures. I grew up reading these stories about Johnny Appleseed, Abraham Lincoln, Nancy Hanks (Lincoln's mother), children caught up in the Indigenous/settler wars, and others.

Alfred Knopf published these books in defiance of the blacklist. *Zapata is Here!*, however, was not published at the time. I remember in the 1990s Meridel talking to me about her disappointment that she could not get *Zapata Is Here!* published. She believed this was because the subject matter, armed war of resistance, was too political for the climate.

I loved the book. It had the poetic imagery that I had become so enamored with in her other books, as well as vivid historical details.

Zapata Is Here! is a coming-of-age story of a young boy who joins Zapata in the fight against the Spanish hacienda system that had taken their land and impoverished them.

One of the most moving parts of the book for me was the demonstration of the importance of literacy in the movement. They had a newspaper that was secretly delivered in markets in small towns, and the boy had to learn to read to know what was going on. Then he became involved in the literacy education of the populace and an important part of the revolution.

It is a good story, exciting, with jailbreaks, battles, and, of course some victories. After the successful election of the president, the banners of Tierra y Libertad (Land and Liberty) that they flew unified the people. The new government did not follow through on the land reform that was a promised part of their rallying cry.

Meeting with Indigenous elders, the Land reform plan was based upon agreements for collective ownership of land that had been developed thousands of years before.

Eventually, the capitalists from the United States exerted their influence on Mexico. Those agents eventually assassinated Zapata.

The story Meridel tells connects directly to today's Landback movements, which are ongoing efforts by Indigenous communities to reclaim traditional lands and lifeways. The modern Zapatista movement in Mexico, too, draws from this same history of collective resistance and radical land reform. I often think about how much Meridel would have loved to know more about them, and how she would have seen this book as part of that continuum.

This book is relevant today. I became determined to see it published. The first step is this volume, edited only for typos and spelling. It is the original manuscript as I believe Meridel would like to have seen it published.

The wonderful folks at the Meridel LeSueur Family Circle and the publishing group, Midwest Villages & Voices, have been very supportive. Enjoy going back to the years of the Mexican Revolution, and imagine how the people in those times were much like us, no wiser, but no more foolish either.

Immerse yourself in those days of Mexico as it fights to come out from Spanish Colonialism. As you turn the page, let yourself be grounded in the words of Meridel's dear friend, the great Minnesota poet Irene Paull, whose tribute to the enduring power of the people feels as timely now as ever.

David Tilsen
Minneapolis, Minnesota, Winter 2025

The People Are a River
by Irene Paull

You can never kill the people
for there always will be more
like the water in the ocean
like the sand upon the shore
you can twist a flowing river
you can choke it with debris
but a river, if its flowing,
it will always find the sea.
You can quench a million fires
but we bear an inner light
like the fireflies that blossom
in the blackness of the night.
You can throw us back to savagery
but when your work is done
our wrath will cut a clearing
through the jungle to the sun.
The wheels that make the world go round
are guided by our hand,
there will always be the people
there will always be the land.

Chapter 1

Timoteo crouching on the bluff above his native village of Anenecuilco heard the lowing of Cleofas, his beloved cow, now a prisoner. Like a person, she was locked up with the other animals in a stockade. He could hear them all crying. "For freedom," he said to his friend Inocencio, his pet frog big as a corn bowl, who was sitting on his big toe, listening to the lowing of the imprisoned animals.

"Yes, they don't like to be locked up behind a barbed wire fence any more than people. Listen," he said, holding up a finger. "I can hear the beautiful voice of Cleofas, who is expecting to be a mother. Oh, let the Virgin look after her!" His mother was trying to raise the twenty pesos to get her out before it was too late. But twenty pesos was a lot of money when a grown man made only one peso for a full day's work.

"You see, Inocencio," Timoteo leaned down to look into the great eyes of the frog that stuck out as if in protest, "My fathers, our fathers, yours too, used to have all this rich land and raised much corn and animals. Oh, my tierra chica, my little earth, how I love thee, and you still belong to us." The big frog said "grrrrrmp" and looked around the stolen land.

It had happened in the night—the arrest of the animals.

"It would be funny if it was not so sad, Inocencio. Yes, to arrest animals who have no pockets to pay the fine. You agree with me, Inocencio? I know you would. It is wicked to arrest animals who have received the blessing of the saints, and Cleofas gives us the milk for our famous cheese we sell at Cuautla. She is like a beloved mother to us. Since papa died, we would starve without her. And now we must go to her rescue."

Yes, it was in the night they had done it.

There was now only one pasture left for the villagers by an ancient spring that had poured water from the steep hills for centuries. The people had been pushed back off their land by the Spanish sugar cane growers, until Timoteo and his mother had to hold their little milpas back by stones, and the grass roof of their adobe hut hit the bluff behind them, as they looked down on the valley which used to be their own.

In this last pasture they had been allowed to take their sheep, goats and cows from which Timoteo and his mother made their living since his father's violent death. They made their famous cheese which they sold at the market in Cuautla where they went every Saturday.

But then in the night secretly, suddenly there was a fence of the new barbed wire, fencing away the green pasture from the hungry bawling animals. The shepherds and the villagers were angry at this but took their animals every night to the strip of green outside. The animals lowing for water pushed against the fence, crying, and the fence gave way. The animals, with the hacienda guards beating them and the army of

Rurales shouting and threatening to shoot them, had simply run to the spring to drink and they all had been arrested. Yes, arrested like people!

"O," Timoteo cried to Inocencio who was making sad noises in his puffed-out body, "If Zapata was here, he would ride and corral our poor animals and gently bring Cleofas, who is with calf, out to mama to care for. He would do this under the noses of the army even. I will not cry, Inocencio. Here, have some water." He poured some water from a gourd into the little clay pot and Inocencio hopped over and stuck his long red tongue into the water and snatched himself a little bug besides.

"There! I heard Cleofas. I can tell her voice anywhere. She is crying 'Come and get me free!'"

He could not bear to think of Cleofas, his beloved cow, crying of hunger. He had many times slept against her warm pelt when the big winds came from the gulf and they spent the nights high in the mountains. She had even licked him with her big tongue tickling him so he laughed and she laughed too. Once she had rolled him in the grass with her horns as if he had been her own calf, as indeed he was. Did she not give him milk and cheese? Many a time he had saved her and her young from the mountain lions that came down in a year of hunger, shooting off firecrackers and keeping a fire going against the wolves.

Then the thought made him shiver. He could not say it to Inocencio even. But he saw clearly—as he saw morning, noon and night—his father's great grass-woven white hat hanging on the wall and his leather-thonged whip and, above them all, his long ancient hunting gun across the low adobe wall. The minute you came in the door you saw them there and expected to see his father eating and his mother serving him and asking what had happened. He never told her right off. It was like a game for he would tell her everything given time, but he liked to tease her. His father's picture too, on the table with the candle burning, with the long mustachios and the great eyes asking Timoteo to always be brave. Do not let them push you too far. Take a stand in the mountains. He saw himself in the night, taking the gun down so not to wake his mama asleep on the petate. But he did not know how to shoot it. That was the trouble. He had to grow to wear his father's hat and, perhaps, to have mustachios like his father and Zapata, to be able to lasso a running horse, and to shoot the bull's eye. Could he be, like Zapata, the greatest charro? Or even known in Mexico City, where he went with the horses of the patron which he trained as no one else could?

He and Inocencio watched down the ravine for his mother, but the sun was going west, throwing the mountain's shadow down upon the village. He knew nothing could make his mother more angry than to have Cleofas, about to have a calf, in such danger. Although his mother was always for peace, no trouble, even against delegations to the government since his papa had not returned from Cuernavaca, found dead in the barrancas.

But Tepepe, the old sheep herder, ought to be down from the mountain with his sheep and goats before the sunset. Timoteo got his education from the old herder, who could not read or write but was wise in the lore of mountain and animal and men and women too.

He did not see his mother, so he lay down with Inocencio under the wall to cool off, and he must have dozed for he was wakened by the tinkle of bells and the curious sound of many sheep and goats pulling the grass in their sharp munching. He saw Tepepe's broad white hat rise up out of the sharp incline, in his white calzones the men wore, the shirt tied in front and the pants tied also. His broad woven hat with ribbons hanging down to keep off rain and sun, to drink from, to use as a basket, a cradle for lamb and child, sat straight across his head showing where the sun stood. Under it, his wrinkled face, as dark as an avocado, sharp eyes that could see for miles and knew every hump and cave of the country, could look into a hurricane, tell the weather, and see things in the past and the future clear as the present.

"So here you are, chico," he said, "having some clear and deep thoughts, I hope." The sheep and goats came through the pass, fanning out behind him and cropping the green of the little shelf that overlooked the river and the village.

"I saw your friends, Alfredo and Anaya, running towards the village without their animals. What were they doing at this hour not shepherding their cows?"

"O, haven't you heard, Tepepe, they have arrested all our animals? All our animals are in jail."

"Arrested!" Tepepe croaked, sitting down so hard that Inocencio jumped three feet into the shade of the cacti. "The animals arrested! I know they are greedy mad for grain, but how can you arrest an innocent animal, one of the creatures of God? How did it happen, Timoteo my son?"

"Well, as you know the haciendados put up the fence with the thorns on it. The animals wanting to drink came close, leaned towards the smell of water, and the fence gave way. They ran, in their thirst, to water, trampling the newly planted cane."

"Beasts are without knowledge, my son, only hunger."

"This I know. If we do not pay, they will keep our animals. Then what will we sell at the market in Cuautla? It is all we have, and Cleofas is about to have a calf."

"Don't tell me more," Tepepe said. "Then the charros came, the little army of Salento, the hacienda owner, riding on fine free horses with guns. They arrested the little cows, sheep, and goats for trespassing in their own pasture, where their sires have fed for hundreds of years since Montezuma and our Aztec grandfathers."

"And that is not all. Twenty pesos to get them out. It is known that nobody in the village can have that amount of pesos. If we do not pay, they will let our precious little animals die!"

"Oh no, they will simply keep them for themselves, the same as they have the land. They planted sugar cane instead of corn so we are the sugar bowl of the world now, but little good it does us." Then Tepepe began to laugh, and it was something to hear him laugh from his lean belly to the eyes that disappeared in his face made of sun and leather. "Arrested!"

he cried, and he looked down in the dust as if something there laughed up at him. "Arrested!" he cried again. His little burro, startled, turned and began to "hee haw hee haw!" and Inocencio darted his red tongue out his wide opening slit across the lower part of his face, his huge eyes blinking.

In the laughter, Tepepe wheezed. "It is well known that animals have no pockets to pay the fine. They will be confused, not being people and not used to being beaten, jailed and even killed as we are. They do not expect to be imprisoned, fined and flogged." Then he was serious, his old lined face like some crag lit now by the evening light, "Oh, it is a misery now. They take our animals, push us off the land, kill our corn and hire our labor to make sugar that goes to a far country and doesn't sweeten our labor." He rose, shaking his great gaunt fist down at the high walls of the hacienda surrounded by the little rock and adobe huts of the villagers.

"We are Indios," he cried, "we are the warriors of Cuauhtémoc who stood against the mighty Spaniard, Cortez." He fiercely took Timoteo by the shoulders and half-lifted him from the ground. "Never forget," he said, "that you are pure Indian. You are pure, and of the greatest people ever known, of the greatest warrior of our land, Cuauhtémoc!"

"We have Zapata," Timoteo was able to say, being shaken like a rattle.

"Zapata, a trainer of horses, a charro, a lady's man of waxed mustachios. Let him become a warrior!"

"Tepepe, you are an orator." Timoteo wished the old man to lose his fierce face and become the pastor again.

"Yes," Tepepe said. "We make great orators because we have so much time alone to think about it. I make many speeches, alas, to the wind."

"Do you think I will ever be wise, Tepepe?"

"Why not?"

"And strong and handsome and rich?"

"He who is not handsome at twenty, strong at thirty, rich at forty, and wise at fifty will never be handsome, strong, rich, or wise."

"Do you think I will be wise? That I would wish more than all. Zapata is the best horseman, the best with the quirt, the best rider and guitar player, but he is also wise with it all."

"Who knows? You are strong."

"You are testing me. I will be like Juárez and Señor Lincoln. He liked so much, strong and wise so nobody could move me to evil."

"You expect the bounty of God wrapped in a tortilla."

"I do not expect God will do it for us. I expect men with God's help."

"God will help. The eye of the Master fattens the goats. I am well burned with years, and I will never be wise."

"You are truly wise, Tepepe, wise with the ways of earth and man. What you know is not known by many. When I learn to write, I will write it all down, everything you say, so you will be known over the whole earth. In the morning, if God lends me life, I will begin to learn. I swear it."

"Not so fast, chico. The haciendados do not wish for you to learn. A dumb ox is the best at the plow. But it is true, the cactus fruit that has been pecked knows best about birds. So you will be the one who will have the suffering and the wounds, and you will have great reason and great power."

"Yes, reason and power and love, like Zapata, for my people. And like him to go every week and open the jails. Shout 'Open up!' and they have to open and let the poor farmers out. Open all the jail doors, all the iron bars, all the fences that keep us out."

"He who with his arms engirdles much can squeeze little," Tepepe said.

"Yes," Tepepe laughed, "I have one, too. He who eats guacamoles and kisses an old woman neither eats nor kisses."

"True, it is true. Alright, chico, tomorrow we will go higher. The grass is fat up there."

"I will stay with you, Tepepe."

"Yes, your little heifers will grow fat this night when the little goats come out, and the three Marys cross the sky, and the Big Dipper tips out its milk. After God, chico, you are next with me. Like my own son who has been lost these years."

Timoteo put out his hand on the burnt brown one.

"You are my only father."

He put Inocencio back into his box and hung him around his neck. The sun went down over the sugar cane that was not theirs. Tepepe in the twilight always opened with memories like the cave of the thieves, strange stories of panthers that led men to water, of charros that turned into ghosts and rode horses of skeleton, of bears that ran away with women, and of Spanish cocks brought over to crow up the dawn. The moon rose on the hill and stood in a clear sky, and the Dipper tipped downward. Tepepe gave Timoteo some tortillas, and Inocencio ate a piece, too.

Tepepe said before taking a bite, "Gracias, Dios, for solid food and an appetite to enjoy until morning, if God so wishes. Amen."

The old Shepard was deep in memory and sorrow.

"Four hundred years we have been their slaves and our heroes have led us against them. Hidalgo just a hundred years ago in 1810, and Morelos and then the great Juárez , and now—"

"Now," Timoteo almost shouted, "Zapata!"

"Zapata?" Tepepe stopped chewing.

"Emiliano Zapata in 1910."

"He can neither read nor write."

"You can read and write later. You have to ride and shoot and dare. Yes, it takes daring to go against the guns of the oppressor. You have taught us that, Tepepe, and Zapata is not afraid. I don't know why, but he is the only one who laughs and does not bend the knee and grab off his hat and bow as if he had been hit in the stomach."

"It is true," Tepepe said. "It is true."

"And if he cannot read, he can talk."

"Like a bird," Tepepe laughed.

"Like an ocelot," Timoteo cried. "Like an angel and a devil, he is with the Spanish and with the Nahuatl." For nearly everyone in Timoteo's village spoke the ancient language of their grandfathers, as well as the language of their conquerors, which was Spanish.

"Ah. yes," Tepepe said, "he speaks with the tongue of the blessed and the possessed. He has a quirt for a tongue, a lash and a fiery heart. You are right, Timoteo. He springs from our soil and our hearts. He is a poor man like us, like Jesús, who springs from our wounds. We are poor, but nourished by our soul, by our ancestors, by time. It is something to ponder."

"You said yourself, men spring from out of the people, and then they fall back into the arms of their mother. The people, if they are true men. You could not buy Zapata, as many leaders have been bought and now themselves have fine haciendas and great flocks of sheep and sugar cane."

"No, you could kill him, but you could not buy him."

"Why doesn't my little mama come? It's getting dark."

They all looked down into the long valley where the smoke now came up from the coke fires on which they were cooking their supper.

"There's mama" Timoteo cried as he saw her begin to climb the path from the barranca to their house. He saw with a sinking heart that Cleofas was not with her. She climbed as if without spirit, as if at last something had dampened her great warm hope that always kept them going and was his only warmth since his father's death and the older children had married.

Tepepe opened one eye from his resting. "No cow," he said and closed his eyes again.

Timoteo saw also his two friends, Anaya and Alfredo, coming slowly over the river. They too looked as if their last friend had been taken from them—all their goats and sheep arrested. You could hear them lowing and crying from this prison and you couldn't help but fear for them. Had they been watered, fed, milked, given fresh hay for the night? What would happen to them? And Cleofas about to calve. She could die of loneliness, she could die of fright.

For the first time he felt an awful fear of something that he understood had caused his father's death. When he had gone to the capital Cuernavaca to protest the seizure of their pasture lands and the theft of their water—and they had killed him. Yes, Porfirio Salento, head of the hacienda, of the lands, of the big sugar mill, it was he.

He started running towards the house, threw open the door and saw his father's big hat, the quirt below and, across above the bed, his father's gun.

Chapter 2

A t the crack of dawn, Timoteo was sliding down the path to the village following the sound of the bleating and lowing animals from the stockades behind the prison. In the Zócalo, he met his friends Anaya and Alfredo, also following the sound of their imprisoned animals.

"They're still locked up," Anaya said as they loped along on their bare feet. Others were also going to see their animals. Anaya was a tall boy, and Alfredo was small like Timoteo. Alfredo said, "I hear Zapata is coming from Cuautla today."

"Good," Timoteo said, "we will have our animals back by milking time."

A high adobe fence surrounded the compound. The boys knew where holes allowed you to look in, but there was only room for one eye. First Anaya looked anxiously for his little goats. Then Alfredo saw his sheep and his four heifers all standing together like frightened friends against the farthest corner of the fence. Anxiously, Timoteo looked for Cleofas. Then he saw her, head down and her big sides panting, her enormous golden eye looking wildly around for friends or enemies. "Sssssssss," he hissed, and he thought she heard him, for she threw up her horned head and blew through her nostrils and looked around wildly.

"She hasn't had her calf yet," he said as they all three squatted in the sand beside the adobe wall. "My mama is almost wild, afraid she will have her calf without attention. We are counting on the fresh milk to make the cheeses for the fair at Cuautla. Oh, if my father was alive, he would go up to Porfirio Salento, and he would say: 'Give me my little cow now. She is a friend of my wife and son,' he would say, 'and we must care for her.' My father had a fierce eye like Zapata, and people did what he said."

Anaya said, "It will take more than that to get our animals out of jail now. My father says that the sugar men are getting bolder and bolder. Salento, remember, is the son-in-law of President Díaz, who will do whatever he says."

"Such a rich man has no use for our flaco animals," Alfredo says. "Why does he want to do it?"

"To frighten us," Anaya said, "to make us feel his power. My father says a man in power has always got to make others feel his power in every way."

It saddened Timoteo not to be able to say what his father might think now. He tried to think of the sayings of his father, but he had been a little boy then—one year ago. He had not become the shepherd he was now, watching the animals for his mother.

"Sssssssss," he hissed once more to Cleofas, but she had gone back to looking at the ground. He could tell everything she was thinking. He cried out, "Cleofas, hold on. I'm here!" A soldier on horseback clattered over to the fence and shouted, "Get away from there or I'll shoot."

The boys ran zig-zagging into the little trees of the river. They washed their feet and threw water on their heads and told each other goodbye, Anaya to watch for Zapata to tell him all that had happened, Alfredo to bring Cleofas up the hill if the animals should by some miracle be released. Timoteo went back to his house so his mother would not be alarmed to waken and find him gone.

She was up and about and angry. "Why do you have to frighten me along with everything else? Oh, men!" she cried, and he smiled for she had called him a man. "You are getting like your father."

He smiled and looked at the picture of his father with his fierce mustachios like Zapata's and his black shining eyes. "Yes, I have his eye," he thought, "when it is fierce enough and has learned to look down the barrel of the gun and can lasso a bull."

As she made their tortillas wrapped around beans and green chili, she kept on complaining.

"Mama, if you would stop," he said, sounding like his father, "that woman's talk, I would tell you that I saw Cleofas, and she said hello to you."

"You saw her, my little friend? How is she? Has she dropped her calf?"

"No, she says she is going to have a splendid calf. She says she will be out by noon, and she has a friend in court to pay her fine."

"Oh, Timoteo, you are such a joker, like your father when he was having it good. Did she look all right? Had she been eating? Did she have water?"

"There was a trough of water there for them and some green straw on the ground. I am sure they had been fed for they were very quiet just looking around for their friends and dodging the flick of a quirt of the horsemen. They have many horsemen looking after them like royalty."

"We must plant the corn in the upper milpas before it is too late," his mother said after breakfast. Since they had lost their lands and corn, they could not feed their oxen and very few had plows. Now they planted in the old way, making a little clearing on the hillside and making a hole with a stick. They dropped the seed into it with a prayer for its nourishment so they would not starve next year.

He walked before his mother and made the hole in the soft ashy earth and she came behind with the precious kernels of corn in her apron. She stooped and dropped one in the hole, and then they both covered it with their brown hands. He said in Nahuatl to please her:

> Dark earth of ours,
> We pray thee.
> Give back the corn we pay thee,
> O holy corn, by moon or morn,

Grow strong, grow tall, grow gaily,
O tierra chica mia.

He ended in Spanish, and his mother laughed. They put the seed in together and covered it.

He kept trying to see over the edge of the hill into the village, which looked very quiet. No signs of Zapata's return which would certainly make a furor. He would come with his brother and other churros, and he would stop at the gates of the hacienda in a flurry of dust. The villagers would run to see what would happen. When he looked over the edge, he saw no sign of Zapata. The women in their shawls were going to the markets or taking their masa in little buckets. His father's old friend came in from the forest with coke to sell, loaded in his burro.

To please him, his mother began to sing the Spanish song of planting, and he joined her. Their two ancient faces with the straight black Indian hair, the strong features and the black slanting eyes were the same that had said the Zapata prayer for corn thousands of years ago:

In the name of God I am planting this seed.
I implore thee to bless my work.
I have thrown you into this field,
And you will remain with my blessing.
And may God free you so we will have something to eat.
Amen.

"Amen," he said.

Tepepe's wizened face rose over the side of the milpas. They both ran to him as if to shake the news out of him. "What has happened to Cleofas?"

Tepepe shook his head. "The sheep, goats and cattle have disappeared. They have simply taken them for their own. Zapata will have something to say to that. In the meantime, I have been all morning without food."

"O, Tepepe, without a woman men starve. Come, we will all eat our comida. The sun says it is time." They went single file down the path to their little house. The mother sat on the bare ground which was the floor. In the old way, she put the corn on the stone metate, which had not changed for thousands of years. She rhythmically swung her body back and forth as with another stone, round as a mallet. She ground the fresh corn into masa, a meal from which tortillas were made. She had some masa dough soaked all night in lime, which she now took, rolled in her brown palms—pat pat pat—slapping the tortillas always into a perfect circle and always of a thinness which made it look like layers of thin dough.

Tepepe man-like squatted in the door in the slant of shade. He told that, when Zapata went with Salento's horses to the city for the races, how their animals were stabled like kings. "Yes," he said, "like kings in palaces with marble troughs, their sides fat and shining, not a shin bone like Timoteo here, running water in every stable."

"Yes, running water and fresh sweet hay four times a day, Zapata told me, and curled and pampered like rich women, and harnessed and made out in silver and engraved leather and plumes and even scented with sweet smelling herbs."

Timoteo and his mother were too astonished for words. Timoteo looked around at the bare house he and his mother had made with their hands, carving the lengthwise kitchen on whose floor they slept on straw mats. They had leveled the earth, wetted it and beaten it down with their bare feet for a floor. Timoteo was proud of the stout clay oven in the corner and the open brazier on which his mother now put the round dough on a metal tin. The clay pots hung on the small logs he and Tepepe had cut and bound together at the corners with maguey fiber they had beat out with their hands. The brush broom he made stood in the corner. There were no windows. Only the opening for the door, but no hinged door. At night, they hung a grass petate over it.

Tepepe's goats had followed him down to the small dirt patio. She now cried out to him not to let the beasts nibble on her nice green plants. Tepepe seemed to make just a little sound, "Psssssst," and the desirous goat left the green leaves and took to the dustier weeds. Tepepe continued his talk which was like the flowing of the Rio Ayala. "Now you see, that goat he has a secreto. He is muy fat, not flaco like the others. They are hunting and chewing like slaves, and he comes along, polite as a fat haciendado. What do you make of it?"

"He has some secret pasture," the mama said, patting and patting the dough.

"Or some ladrino is fattening him to steal him later," Timoteo said, stirring the beans over the charcoal fire of the brazier.

"Not likely," Tepepe said.

"Are the other cattle jealous?" Mamacita asked.

"Jealous? No, they are not politicos. They are innocent sheep of our Lord."

"Oh, excuse me, Tepepe," she laughed.

Timoteo was excited. "Maybe that is the secreto of Zapata. He has some green pasture of courage to feed on that the rest of us have lost. We have become slaves bent in the middle, frightened. But here comes a man who is fat with courage, who bows to no one even for food."

Tepepe was a little offended. "We all have courage. I am a shepherd. I have my own courage. There is a line I will not cross over in order to live. I have my dignity."

"Yes, it is true, Tepepe, but Zapata is like a horn blowing the Diana. He rouses us all. We remember our courage. We remember everything, the long years, the death of our fathers, and even how our children must have freedom, must not be slaves. Land means freedom. Our land back and freedom."

"Aye," Mamacita cried, "he is talking about his coming children already!"

"My father must have thought of me when he was brave at Puebla, going to Cuernavaca on the committee. It takes much courage for your children to stand naked, a white rabbit, before the guns of the foxes."

"That it does," Tepepe said, "And it will be the pastors who will make an army, coming down from the hills. You, my son,

are also a shepherd as was that Good Shepherd who never let a
sheep be lost. The pastors are before kings, out there with your
flock you are nobody, but you are never forgotten. All nature
remembers you. It is lonesome. Your book is open. Your book
is the earth and the sky. Every man for his own saint, and every
spider for his own web, and every pastor for his own herd and
pasture. We are not without ceremonies, not without councils.
Let the oppressors remember that, and much bears our name.
The pan de pastor made of corn and water and salt we made up
in our lonely need. We have a leafy table, the earth. The fattest
goat is known as the cabra de pastor and he, like the pastor, has
an instinct to be the finest goat and not a jicara—a water cup, or
a fine lacquered gourd, or even veal. He remains a goat and is
glad as I remain a pastor under this morning star and nobody
can call us his man. I am my own and my Lord's, and I know
that kidding must come in the light of the moon or many die."

"Yes," Mamacita said. "It will be towards the full moon
at the end of the week and my poor Cleofas a prisoner. Oh, if
papa was only here, only alive now. That's what comes of your
committees. Better to be quiet and live."

"Oh, Mama!" Timoteo cries, "Don't say that. Papa would
never say that. You know he would say a man has to fight
sometime."

Tepepe looked at her under his brows ashamed, and
she gave the tortilla an angry pat, and Timoteo put his arm
around her bent shoulders.

"We have Zapata now. He has power among the
haciendados. He will have some influence over President
Díaz."

She shook his hand off her shoulder. "Oh, Zapata, that young upstart. You men always think of committees and people of influence. That's what they said to your poor father when he went to the Governor of Morelos to try and save our fruit trees. Then they had to send a committee after him to find him with eight bullet holes in his body."

They let her cry. And now she cried, "Cleofas, my poor cow, like a woman friend she was to me, with the same woes. We will never get her back now she has disappeared. Never, never will we get back the land of our fathers."

"Now, now, woman, don't cry. It is not a time to cry. Díaz will perhaps have to show a heart."

"Of stone," she cried, "of stone."

"Don't say that, Mamacita. Papa used to say the people will fight sometimes, somewhere and get their land back and their life back."

"Yes, Timoteo, you are becoming the talker your papa was. A wise one. I should have two wise and strong men, my husband and my son." She made him itch kissing him, and he took Inocencio out of his box.

"Kiss him, Mamacita, he loves kissing."

"Aye," she cried, "that little monster with the owl's eyes." He pretended to come at her with the big-eyed Inocencio, and she laughed and ran, leaving the prints of her bare feet on the floor. He ran after her laughing, holding up the frightened Inocencio until they both were out of breath, laughing.

"True, true, isn't it, Inocencio? No one can stay on their knees." Timoteo had set him down and he was jumping for crumbs and grrrmped "True. True."

"And you, Tepepe, didn't mention the hitch called the amarrado de pastor even at sea and the coyotillo bush that sticks its thorns in goats and must be known, as well as the Guyacan bush that gives animals the creeps and drives them crazy. And the milk of the Golondrina weed in the thorn sores is a very bad thing. You may not know how to read in a book, but you know how to read all signs of wolves and ocelots and signs of storm and even of earthquake and volcano."

"Yes," said Tepepe. "It is such that we know but we are blind and dumb. We could give many things to the world. We could teach how to fight the Rurales lying low and how to evade them and drive them crazy. Our knowledge could be used."

"Oh, you men." Mamacita bustled around them, putting the hot tortillas filled with the filling beans in their hands. "Wash," she cried, "we are not animals. Look at those hands." Timoteo and Tepepe dipped the ends of their fingers in the bowl she offered them of precious water. "Oh, the water is not possessed. What would you do without women?"

Tepepe peered at her with his cunning eyes. "What would we do indeed?" and he gave her a sly pat as she passed, which sent her blushing and scurrying to the safety of her grinding the corn on the metate.

"So," Tepepe said, "Be proud of being a pastor. Be proud of being an Indio. Say after me: 'I am pure Indian. I speak my own language and not the language of the conquerors. I am proud.'"

Timoteo repeated it after him, and Mamacita hid her face for the tears of pride on it. It was a chant in Nahuatl and brought to her being dim memories of the great cities of Monte Albán of which she had heard, the great city upon which the capital was built of Tenochtitlan, one of the great cities of the earth, a city of grand architecture, of music, dancing, astronomy, philosophy. It was from this great people they had come and were still a part.

She heard her son: "I am pure Indio. I speak the language of my people. We have been Indian for thousands of years. We have a great past and a great future. We are not afraid."

Someone was shouting from below the hill. It was Alfred. "Zapata!" he cried, "is coming. He's drawing up to the gates of Salento's hacienda. Now there will be all hell to pay. Come! Come! Timoteo."

"Come, Mamacita," Timoteo urged, taking her hand, but she drew back.

"No, no," she cried. "No, I want no trouble with that young Zapata. He will ruin us all." And she drew back, flinging her hands out.

Timoteo turned and ran swiftly behind Alfredo. Tepepe suddenly seemed to have the legs of a young buck, and he ran after, in his famous lope which covered miles of mountains and desert, without tiring.

The whole village was running, crying, "It's Zapata! Zapata is here!"

Chapter 3

When they got down to the Zócalo, the dust was stirred under the running feet of the villagers and the prancing horses drawn up sweating from what must have been a swift ride from Cuautla. Salento had come out on his finest Arabian horse and at first had tried to persuade Zapata to calm down. They were friends. Didn't Zapata train his fine-bred horses and look after his great stables?

"Why, man, they were friends, weren't they?" Zapata's horse seemed to be making circles around Salento's, which made him nervous as Zapata shouted: "Now you have imprisoned the animals of my people, whose lives depend upon the milk and meat and cheese. What are you thinking of? You want to get them back in the fields at a slave pittance, to beat them back as you did a few years ago when you destroyed their orchards so they would have no fruit. You have taken the corn milpas, and now they will have no meat!"

"Oh, don't get excited," Salento said, whose horse was frothy and sweating surrounded by these circling rebels. "You know well I have a deed for this land from the King of Spain."

He should not have said hat. A great cry went up, and Zapata seemed to grow six feet tall sitting on his horse.

"What King!" he roared. "This was our land when all Europe was a jungle. We had the mother calendar, the telling of time, measurement of the stars when your race was living in caves." A strange, frightening laugh rose from the women.

Timoteo and his two friends stood close together, the dust flying in around them, and sometimes had to back away from the hips of Zapata's fine horses.

"You can get your animals," Salento said, "only twenty pesos for their keep."

The crowd moaned. Zapata shouted: "You pay a man one peso for a full day's work. How can he bail out his cattle for twenty? You will force us to send a committee to Díaz."

At this it was the time for Salento to laugh, being the brother-in-law of Díaz, married to his sister. All the villagers knew this well. They had once gotten a full stomach at the wedding, all free.

Salento turned his horse to the iron gates of his hacienda. "That's all I have to say, Emiliano. You'd better calm your people down!" Inside, they could all see a regiment of Rurales mounted and armed.

Anaya began to jump up and down, shouting something, and Alfredo, red-eyed, was running with the crowd to the Zócalo. Timoteo ran too, and they all gathered around Zapata, who got down off his horse and stood on a bench to speak to his people.

The man who was called the little Ink Pot, because he was the only one in the village who could read and write, climbed up beside him. Montana, the school teacher from Cuautla who also could read and write, stood beside him. The boys got themselves through the crowd to stand by the tallest man, a miner, name Andrea Fuentes, a northern man who was taller than any of the village of Anenecuilco, whose people were small from five hundred years of hard work and poor food.

Zapata held up his hand, and it was so quiet you could hear the animals asking for their supper and their friends.

"We will elect now a committee to catch the night train to Mexico City. We will take our grievances to President Porfirio Díaz himself. It has gone on long enough and arresting the animals is the last."

A roar of assent went up.

"Who shall go?" he said. They were very used to democratic procedures, for their land was held in common, planted in common, and their councils, old as the Mayan traditions, were elected and sat for the good of the people and took care of their affairs.

The names were called out, and it was apparent at once who the committee should be. The Ink Pot was the first, of course, for he could read and write down what happened. And the next was Montana, who also could make good speeches and write proclamations and looked good among the intellectuals, being a school teacher himself. Then someone cried out the name of Fuentes, for he was so large and strong he made an excellent bodyguard and could get you off and on trains, and through the enemies of Mexico City, which was a place they rarely visited, although it was but a short distance over the mountains past the old volcano Popocatépetl.

Then the name of Pablo Penales and Orozco and of course Emiliano's brother, Eufemio, and Emiliano himself. "Let's see, they counted," "It is enough—a good committee!"

Now they had something to do. They all surrounded the committee. They would all contribute their best clothes. You had to look good to appear before the President. The women were already thinking of who had shoes, socks, city pants, coats—for you could not go in the white cotton loose pants and shirts the men of those parts wore. Zapata, they knew, would look like a fashion plate, for no man in the world could look more dashing, stylish, and still wear the beautiful image of the pure Indian.

The three boys waited, running about the Zócalo like mad crickets to see who would be wearing what, who would appear first. There were only two trains a day to the city and they had only a few hours to catch the last night train.

It was not only the men who dressed up, but the girls and young women began appearing in their best shawls and brightest skirts. Even the old women, wound in style in their black rebozos, remembering old days and old committees when they were young and ripe and remembered also, as they all did, some times when the men did not come back, when the committees simply disappeared or were shot or imprisoned or nothing was ever heard of them.

"Look, look," the boys shouted, as Pablo appeared, thrust out of someone's coat, probably taken off a dead man in the old war in Puebla their fathers had fought. Every house had some strange Spanish grandee's coat or stockings or even shoes kept from the old wars.

Tall Pablo jutted out of his Spanish coat, and his hair had been slicked down by some woman, wetted and clung black to his head. He laughed at himself trying to pull his arms into the short sleeves and pull it down over his muscular body. Anaya, laughing, pulled the coat sleeves. "Maybe it will grow on you," he said, "give way and cover you."

"Why he looks fine," Timoteo said, "very fine. And look, this kind of coat has many pockets in which you can carry many things."

"Bring us back something in the small pockets— something small," Alfredo said. Some little girls began to hold hands and dance around him. He stood smiling and then it was seen that his poor feet were in a stiff pair of military shoes. Everyone wondered how he would ever walk or sit on his horse in the tight pants.

"I'll do that," he said, "just let down the suspenders." They examined these curious red elastics that held the pants up.

Then appeared the Ink Pot, a small man with huge eyes, and he sometimes put upon his nose a pair of iron-rimmed glasses and peered out of them, but this was only for documents of importance. He also had a coat on and a strange thing intellectuals wore called a tie, which went like a noose around the neck and was tied and was often black as in mourning. Nobody could understand its uses but it was fashionable and those who came from Mexico City for parties at the hacienda wore these, so they were proud to have the Ink Pot represent them in this way.

Montana and Andrea Fuentes wore some kind of work clothes the miners brought to the village, a loose kind of jean, and they carried their blankets for coats.

"This is the way we look," Fuentes said, "and they can like it or not. We should go in our white calzones, just as we are, to represent ourselves. I'm against dressing up like the monkeys we are going to see!"

Some agreed with this and laughed. Timoteo and his friends did not know. It was like reading. Did you need it? What did you need?

Last came the two Zapata brothers, and they both wore their elegant charro costumes, their huge cartwheel hats. The girls and boys ran to touch them as they mounted their horses, and there were jokes about the girls of the city and how they would never see them again. The city would get them. There was laughter and wonderful relief.

"Be back tomorrow," they cried as men always cry going off on a journey.

And just as the dust was settling, Timoteo saw his mama standing back in the dark, her shawl around her head, her face burning in anxiety and hope, with old memories and fears, and her loneliness and her hard working came to him in the instant of seeing her after the hoofs had died out. The women and girls turned back to their houses full of children and light, and beans cooking and the tortilla smelling of good corn.

Anaya and Alfredo went to their fathers' houses where the children were still young, and Timoteo ran swiftly to his mother, putting his arm around her as he had often seen his father do.

"Mamacita," he cried, "wasn't it grand? Now you will believe in committees. They will return, you will see. Díaz will give us our animals back and see that we get paid for work in the sugar cane."

"Oh, Díaz," she said, glad to feel him so close. "Men in power are all the same."

"Did you see Zapata, Mamacita? He can sit a horse like nobody, rope a calf or do the pass of death so fine, so timed, jumping from a running horse to throw a bull by tail or horn. And for speaking, why I bet he can read!"

"I saw Zapata," she cried into the dark of the hill as they climbed home, "but I saw your father and I need to see no other man!"

"Oh, Mamacita, was he handsome as Zapata?"

"There was no man sat on a horse as he did. When he returned from the battle of Puebla, riding through the sun, triumphant he was, and free."

Timoteo wanted to say, "And could he read?" But he was afraid to hear the answer, and what was reading anyway? It couldn't be much if neither his father nor Zapata could read. What was reading anyway? What did you know? What did you learn that you needed? He did not know and he ran in to light the candle under his father's picture, so his mother would not stumble and so it would be warm and light for them there in the night.

Chapter 4

The next day was the most frightening of any day Timoteo had ever spent in his life, except the day they brought his father home from the barranca, his breast full of holes. They counted eight bullets.

There was no work. The mill was shut down. All work in the fields had ceased. The army of the Rurales, mounted, stood all day behind the hacienda walls. You could hear the horses neighing, or a command or the rattle of sabers or cocking of guns.

The three boys went round and round the walls. Timoteo at first could not see Cleofas. Then he found her, with his one eye pressed to the hole, clear over by herself behind the trough. She was breathing heavily and, as he watched, she lay down, head on her flank and closed her eyes. As long as she was lying down, she shouldn't have the calf. He made a prayer. "Don't let her have the calf 'til tomorrow."

By then, the committee would surely have returned and the animals been ransomed. He could not, in his wildest imagination, have imagined what really would happen to free them and what such a little action could start.

Then something more terrible happened. About noon, they circled around the spring and the meadow, just to see how the barbed wire fence was standing up. They all three stopped as something glinted at the end of the meadow where the trees followed the river Ayala. They didn't speak. They looked. Then Anaya said, startled: "Machine guns!"

They dared not go closer, but they could see they were like little cannons, the kind mounted on Zócalo in Cuautla, only they were smaller. It was said that they could fire many rounds in a minute and kill dozens of men without reloading.

"Machine guns!" they all said. "They are going to keep our animals out of the meadow, and keep us out, who are the same as animals to them."

"Yes," they agreed. Awed, they went back to the village. "We better not say anything. Some old woman picking greens will discover them soon enough. It will put the whole village in a panic. Let us not say anything until the committee returns."

"Maybe we should tell the council," Anaya said. "Maybe they should be armed, ready."

"Wait," Alfredo said, "Wait a little while. Nothing will happen at noon."

"Why not at noon?" Anaya laughed. "You should attack always, I have heard, when the enemy least expects it?"

"Well, the enemy now is having its nap and so are we."

They walked through the village. The little stores were dark, fragrant, cool. They had no money to buy anything. The mountain river ran cool in the afternoon, and they sat with their feet in the water. It was so still. Not even Cleofas was crying out.

The patio of the house of an old family was a place the little Ink Pot had brought some books for them to look into, and he was always telling them they must learn to read, to find out what was in the great books of the world. In the summer, he often appeared in the pastures and sat with them, pointing out the letters and drawing them in the dust with a stick. The boys learned to spell out "Anaya" in the dust, "Alfredo," and "Timoteo," but what good was that? No one ever wrote to them, only called them to come and bring the water, take the sheep to the mountain, plant the corn, and they didn't write their names, they only called them. They never saw them spelled out on any mountain or in water or in stones.

There was the big book the little Ink Pot had left in the abandoned house, and anyone could come and lay it down, open it up, and look at the pictures and the mysterious hieroglyphs beside them. You did not know what they said. It was the *Illustrated History of Mexico*, including Montezuma, the Mayans, and thousands of years before that—of the Zapotecs and those that spoke their language, the Nahuatl, that perhaps was never written but passed down from the mouth, the voice, like song.

That's what the word was to them, shout, caress, song, command, grief, history told by father to son, mother to child.

What wrote it down and who made what is called a book?

"This is a book," Anaya said. "There are many books." They leaned over the book open at a page showing ancient pyramids of their people. "Yes there are whole buildings, I have heard, with nothing but books."

"What is in them?" Alfredo asked. "How do you make a book?"

"O there is much in them," Timoteo said. "Now, if you could ever get the meat out of this book, you would know a good deal. Here it shows how we are an old race, older than the blancos. Yes, much older. We had mathematics, philosophy. These are words Tepepe taught me. He makes collections of words to say over at night in the rainy season. Now, here you see Cuauhtémoc. He shows how to fight. After Montezuma gave in to Cortez, Cuauhtémoc fought to the last man right down the streets of Mexico, then called Tenochtitlan. Now there was a great city. They had huge markets. Cortez said it was the most beautiful city he ever saw, and he had seen the cities of his own country, I guess. Never forget that's where we come from."

They turned the pages to other pictures of battles, of the face of a white-haired man plunging forward, and they all knew his face. Hidalgo who had revolted against the Spanish in 1810, ringing the bells and crying "Death to all Spaniards!" He had taken over one state and was outside Mexico City when he was captured and beheaded, and his head hung on a post for all to see.

"Now here," Timoteo said, "is Juárez and the other face behind him you see, that is the North American Abraham Lincoln that Juárez loved so much. Yes, he wanted Justice. Like Juárez, the law. That's what Juárez said: the same law for all."

"And now, not in the book yet, there is Zapata."

"Zapata. Will he be a hero?"

"Of course. Maybe he will be president. You never think so at the time. Juárez was a poor country Indian boy none of the boys would speak to. He had no airs. He was an Indian like us."

"How do you know so much, Timoteo, who can't read?"

"I listen" Timoteo said. "And I can tell if anyone knows something. I am like a root. I put myself down in their soil and I draw up everything I can."

"You are a ladrón, a thief," Anaya laughed.

"Yes, of knowledge. But you cannot steal knowledge. It is for anyone who can get it."

"Do you think we will ever know anything?"

"Of course. We know a lot now. We learn from the earth, from having to find food, from having to fight."

Just then, Tepepe came in and out of the heat of the noon, leaving his burro and goats outside lying down in what shade they could find. "Hours until the evening train," Tepepe said, "and not a sign of the animals. They have taken them as their own, as they take everything."

"No," Timoteo cried, "they cannot do that. You will see when the committee returns, you will see! As you say, Tepepe, it takes time for the barefoot to get a hearing with those in shoes."

Anaya laughed. "We are like horses, shod only for races and fiestas, only horses don't go on committees, though they should."

Timoteo looked down at his own bare dusty feet that had never known a shoe, only the piece of rubber tire he tied to them when he went to the Stoney Mountains.

"Will the Presidente see them? Will it be too late for our poor animals?"

Tepepe squatted on his heels, took from him his handful of cacahuates (peanuts), passed them around to the boys, who squatted beside him. Inocencio sat on a rock, listening as usual to the wisdom of the old shepherd. "As the Moro said to his master, after he got the burro over the barranca. Every king to his kingdom! This is our problem, the animals, and the Presidente has his and they are never the same problems. The wolf and the lamb have different problems."

"Well, you often say, Tepepe, that you are a king."

"Yes, of my pastures. I am a pastor, and, as you know, the King Jesús welcomed first in the manger the pastor with his kine. The goats and lambs and the shepherds greeted him and watched over him. I have seen it. You have seen it. The saviours of the race are always without a place to lay their heads."

"Oh, we should have sent you, Tepepe, on the committee," Anaya said. They loved the old shepherd who gave them lessons in how to live, how to endure, how to learn from the book of the earth and the skies and the heart of man.

"You would be splendid as a flag on a committee," Alfredo said, cracking a peanut.

"There is great danger on a committee," Tepepe said, and they listened to him remembering the terrible thing that had happened to Timoteo's father.

"Yes, there is danger when the humildes ask something of the powerful. Coming out of the palace, you can be shot, by mistake they say, while escaping or not stopping soon enough."

Tepepe assured them. "Nothing of the kind with Zapata, friend of Salento, with three pueblos in it, and the Ink Pot to write everything for the papers. It's different when you can write."

"Is it different? What good is writing?"

"What good!" growled Tepepe. "Only the ignorant make such a sound. The word speaks to others, the written word can be where you are not, and speak to thousands, yes, even millions. The word of our saviours comes down to us on the paper. Hidalgo, 'Death to all Spaniards,' someone wrote that down when he said it, so we would hear it through time, a hundred years. And the words of Juárez right in this book. I cannot read them, but someone like Montana or the Ink Pot could read them to us, and our minds would grow larger. Word is more important than the gun."

The boys listened, awed by his severe intense passion. They looked into the book, at the signs.

"Reading and writing," Anaya said, "that is one of the things we will be fighting for!"

"Yes," Alfredo said. "Reading and writing."

Said Timoteo: "I can't understand it, but I will learn."

Tepepe's burro came in the door and began to eat some grass growing out of the crumbling walls of the adobe.

"Yes," Anaya said, "we should have sent you, Tepepe. What would you have said?"

"Well, first, you must not get shy of the gold chairs, the curtains, the grandeur, and the high manners of those in power. They put them all on to make you feel lower than a snake."

"Now," Alfredo said. "Show us how the committee will act. Let the jackass there be Díaz and tell us what will be said."

They all laughed, thinking of the burro being Díaz, with his poor shaggy coat full of dust, and the burro looked around comically, too, as if saying "What's going on here? I refuse to be President."

Tepepe rose and soothed down his old calzones. "Señor Jackass, I mean President, Señor Díaz. We come from the State of Morelos and we are hungry and discouraged. They took away our corn lands many years ago, and now they have arrested our animals, who have no pockets and no credit to pay their fines. It's no use to push this committee aside, Señor. The son of the shepherd killed coming from Cuernavaca, his animals have been stolen also."

Timoteo's jaw tightened. "Will he mention my father, our name?"

"Most likely," Tepepe said. "Zapata has a map of everyone whose land was stolen, who fought against it, who was whipped, humiliated. All are in his mind in a list."

"In his heart, he remembers all." Timoteo said.

"In his great wild heart," Tepepe said. "See, my burro is nodding his head now waiting for the report, already knowing what he will say."

"What will he say?" the boys asked in unison.

"What do jackasses say? 'Hee haw and my name is mud.' Zapata will stand there. 'The Rurales molest us,' he will say, 'carry off our girls, take our crops, do the dirty work of the haciendados. Señor, we fought in the reform and put you into power. We fought against the French. My grandfather was killed at Pueblo. Do not be impatient to right the wrongs of our people,' Díaz will say, having another sip of wine."

Here Tepepe took the old earthen cup, crooked his finger comically and pretended to drink. Just then, the donkey shook his head up and down, wanting a drink too, and brayed, "Hee haw—hee haw!"

"Yes, yes," Tepepe looked down the hawing mouth. "Yes, it is true. He says that justice often has been given by a jackass!"

"Hee haw," said the burro. "Yes, it is true." Tepepe lifted the long dirty burro ear and shouted into it.

They all laughed. Timoteo, entering into the spirit of the pantomime, strutted up blowing out his cheeks, like Pablo in his tight suit. He stammered, pulled down his coat, spun his hat around, and imitated Pablo.

"Truly the price of sugar rises but the poor workers get not one centavo more, even less an hour. When the crop is bad, it is not the rich who lose, but it is taken out of the hides of the poor so the rich never lose."

Anaya stepped forward as Zapata. "The little Ink Pot, he will tell about the raw land, how it has been taken from us, cleared for sugar cane and leaving us no grazing land, no water—and half the crop to the landlord, come drouth or worm."

"Oh, our committee looks grand," Tepepe said, "talks like a whirlwind, bold as a lion, cunning as a fox," and Tepepe leaned against the wall to sleep and the burro became a burro again, and they all waited.

By four o'clock, someone had discovered the guns by the river. The cry went up. A line formed facing the guns. Never before had this happened in their village, men squatting behind this demon gun that they knew could mow down a village of men, women, and children in one terrible sweep.

They stood. They were waiting. The committee would come on the afternoon train or perhaps not until the following morning. Who could know? Only the hacienda had a telephone and no message would come from there, they were sure.

People came in where Tepepe and the boys waited. Some brought tortillas and beans, and soon there was a glowing circle squatting around the book, waiting.

Timoteo brought down his mother, for it was lonely up on the hills, and he had taken her to the hole in the wall. She had looked through and at last had seen Cleofas still with her heavy burden. "Wait, wait," she cried. "Try to wait. I will help you soon."

"They are feeding the animals," Tepepe said, "never fear. They are worth money. They are property. Now they are their property, and they will be fed in a way you, my poor friends, could never feed them. And don't worry. They will use the good rich milks and, even if it suits them, butcher a few of them for their tables. Oh, they are not going to waste anything that is worth money. No, my friends!"

The village waited all that night, and the committee did not return. Vigil lights burned before the saints. The moon came up and made the animals cry for their friends and homes. Ghosts seemed to float through the village all night, and little bonfires flamed along the river as they waited, trying to still old fears and old memories.

Chapter 5

That night, the three boys drifted through the village like smoke, dodging the Rurales who clattered around the Zócalo every hour to see that the villagers had all gone into their houses for the night.

The people of the village were all invisible but they watched everything that was happening. Everything was still. Even the animals seemed to feel the menace of the machine guns, which anyone creeping up to the barbed wire could see glint now and then in the darkness.

"There is a soldier behind each one," Alfredo said.

"And there are six of them," Anaya said.

"And they could mow down the whole town," Timoteo said. "In one blast. One round. One aim."

"We'll figure not to be in front of them," Anaya said.

"I never thought they would do that, setting up guns in our own meadows, blast them to hell," Timoteo said.

"Easy, shepherd," Timoteo roused from his sleep. "Easy now."

Anaya said, "It fills you up. You have to spit it out. How many centuries does it take for you to get filled up with insult, theft, hunger?"

"Chin up," Alfredo said. "Swallow it, my father says, and let it fill you up and get at it. Don't let it poison your spirit, he says."

"They will not get me," Timoteo said, clenching his fists. "I will not be mowed down, as they say, as if we were bad corn or wild animals, or sugar cane. No, let them set up their guns and point at us 'til kingdom come, 'til Cuauhtémoc rises from the dead."

"Ah," Tepepe said fondly, "They have lost three of their slaves this night. I can see that without any light from the stars."

The three boys looked at each other. It was true they had changed. Something about the machine guns pointed at them made it different."

"How many are there, Anaya?" Tepepe asked.

"Six," he answered, "with six soldiers manning them and pointed straight at the village."

"Six," Alfredo said. "Could six good men come up from behind them in the dark, one for each man and each gun, and strangle them? Could they, Tepepe?"

"Well, it is not impossible. No, it is possible. But let us sleep and save our strength. Always sleep the instant the marching and the shooting stops. Get your strength. Hoard your strength. Don't let it out, as water out of a half empty bottle, with talk either. Just rest and wait 'til morning and the struggle begins again."

But it was impossible to sleep. The boys in their new bravery huddled together, their eyes wide open on the day that would come, and what it would bring. They felt each other in a different way. They let their arms fall upon each other. They let their cheeks touch the cheek of their brother warrior. Like ripening pears, they hung in the dark, close to each other, ripening together. And the old shepherd sent out the strong courage of his own heroic life.

The whole village waited, no longer able to hear the lowing of their animals, no longer hearing anything. All was still, the guns pointed. The Rurales with a great clatter patrolled the village every hour, nervously feeling that, instead of keeping watch, it was they who were being watched.

In the morning, the people all tried to go about the business of the day in the usual manner, ignoring the soldiers, the guns pointed still at the village, the silence of their arrested animals and the old fear that came back to them from the four hundred years of living under the armies and authorities of the conqueror.

Timoteo went with Tepepe and with the goats to the mountain. Alfredo and Anaya had to look after the animals that were left to them and help their fathers, who pretended to be working at the river making a dam, but only to keep an eye on the guns and the Rurales. It was hard to look normal. Timoteo could look down from the hill, and they had an arrangement that Anaya or Alfredo should signal from the river if anything was heard of the committee arriving in Cuautla.

Tepepe seemed coiled in himself like a snake, but Timoteo knew he heard every sound and could hear the hoof beats of horses through his own body miles away. About noon, Tepepe got up. Timoteo knew every sound of a barking dog, a hoot owl, a crow, and every change in rhythm had a meaning. He listened with Tepepe. He tried to hear through his feet any sound of horses' hoofs within the earth. He knew by Tepepe's face that he heard them coming. He seemed to feel a change in the village below. Men stopped work. The dogs listened. Then a cry seemed to ascend from the village, and, at the same time, people were running towards the road. You did not so much hear it as feel it on your skin, a far faint movement coming up out of the dust and now communicated to everyone. Even the horses neighed, whinnied, stamped.

Timoteo began to run past his mother who had appeared in the doorway. Tepepe seemed to spring up in his very bones, badly hinged, but powerful and spry. They both sprinted down the path, seeing at the same time Zapata ahead coming at full speed and the others behind him, kicking up a cloud of light and dust and shouts.

Timoteo found himself running alongside Alfredo and Anaya, who turned their faces to him shouting something, but he could hear nothing but the thud of running horses towards the Zócalo. They all reached the tiny park at the same time, the Rurales reining their horses and surrounding them so you felt for a moment it was a trap. But the boys pushed into the crowd and saw the familiar gleaming dusty faces of the committee looking quite different than they had when they set out. Pablo's dusty coat was hanging from the saddle horn. The little Ink Pot looked like he had a fever, hanging to his big horses, squinting without his glasses. There was Fuentes and Montana without his black noose tie, and Zapata and his brother waving their big hats to the people and smiling as if something wonderful had happened.

The boys looked at each other, smiling reassured. Something wonderful beyond all telling must have happened.

"Pouf," said an old woman. "It's the light of tequila you see. They have been drinking as everyone does in the city."

"Hush," the boys said severely. "Listen to what they have to say."

"Sssssss shhhhhhhh," the people all turned, warning each other. "Quiet. Quiet."

They saw Zapata dismount. Timoteo was struck with envy when it was Alfredo who sprang to hold his horse, and the people took his elegant legs in embroidered pants, lifted him, and carried him to the bandstand. Zapata held up his hand and said Montana would be chairman. He was always chairman. Although he was short, he was powerfully built for a teacher and had a big voice that could be heard and demand order. He had a habit of making long speeches, though, and the people were wary.

They all wanted to hear what had happened and what would happen here and now in their time, in this village, to these beloved animals which gave them life. As usual, Montana began eloquently telling how the hacienda, large as any country in Europe, would have to listen to the whole population that had been made slaves to sugar. But when he started back in history to the priest, Father Hidalgo, and they knew he would then come to Juárez and how Díaz grabbed the country with speculators in oil and how he was not the puppet of the landowners, they groaned. They were always glad to get a glimpse of this history, but now they cried, "What about our animals?"

"Cleofas," Timoteo heard himself shouting, "is expecting a calf."

Everyone named the name of his own animals as if they were imprisoned people dear to them.

Zapata held up his arms. His face gleamed in the sun, sweated as if of shining bronze. His eyes always flashed straight into you so deep, fiery and alive, like the eyes of the young Cuauhtémoc must have flashed, when alone he opposed Cortez and fought him street by street.

"We have something to tell you that you never dreamed of," Zapata shouted.

"What news? Tell us, Emiliano! Tell us. Let Zapata speak!" The cry went up, as if from the very hills. "Zapata, Zapata! Zapata! Viva! Viva Zapata!"

Montana pushed Zapata forward. He stood there for a moment, a little awkward, and then when he spoke he was like silk, quick and powerful.

"Díaz taunted us," he said. " 'Go ahead and have an election,' he told us, 'and see if you can win. You are free to do that.' He forgets he is an Indian. He has dyed his hair and wants to change his skin. His tables are groaning with food. He is dressed like an emperor. But there is something happening. We found this out. It is not only to us. We are not the only ones."

"But something is happening to us," and many began to shout out about how they had been arrested for kilning lime on their own land, another for hunting in his own hills. Now with the cattle imprisoned. It's Señor Díaz who sent word to have the spring and pasture guarded.

A shepherd shouted out: "Yes, the guns are mounted along his pasture. I saw them this morning. Machine guns."

"Guns," Zapata cried. "Already in the meadow?"

"Yes, yes!" they shouted. The committee looked shocked and angry.

"We will see about guns in our old meadow and men and animals in prison!" Zapata cried again. "Now the little Ink Pot has something to say."

The Ink Pot had a high, penetrating voice, and he was waving a paper—what was called a newspaper—which came only from the city, and they were silent to hear.

"This paper," he said, "has news for you," and he told how they got the newspaper. After they left Díaz, they felt lower than a snake's belly. Díaz would promise them nothing. "Then our dandy Pablo here," Pablo looked up, surprised. He was taking off his shoes. "Yes, he had to have his shoes shined, and the person who shined them put this into his boot. This paper—"

Everyone groaned. That was the problem with those who had the words, they spoke so many of them and at all times, completely hiding the real information. You always had to wait.

"And on the train, we read this paper, and this paper tells us that we are not alone. It tells that people all over Mexico are rising up against President Díaz."

"Rising against Díaz?" There was a lively buzz.

"Yes." He pointed to the mysterious words. "Here it tells how the miners of Sonora and the farmers of La Paz have formed an army." He turned the page, so excited that he dropped one. "The silver miners, the Tarahumaras. are revolting. It says the miners of San Luis Potosi are staying out of the mines, arming themselves. It says the fishermen of Santa Cruz are striking. It says the women in the mills of Puebla laid down in front of the trains so they could not get the goods out. And, my friends and brothers, you may not believe it, but it tells about the sugar workers around the sugar mills of Cuautla. It tells about us! It names us. We are written down on the paper."

They all pressed closer and hands stretched out to touch the mysterious paper they could not read. Timoteo was struck suddenly as if by a big light. To think of it—how is it possible? The word to open the doors of ignorance. The Ink Pot was answering the unasked question of where this paper that knew so much came from. He was saying, "It is published by a man you never heard of. I have never heard of. Ricardo Flores Magón, who had to flee to a place in the United States on the Mississippi River called—"

Montana filled him in. "St. Louieeeee," he said. "How this paper gets down to Mexico City and is stuck in the boot of Pablo de Morales, I don't know, but it is a friend to us."

"What is it called?" someone cried out.

"It is called *Regeneración*. It means to live again, like the resurrection of our Lord Jesús."

There was a silence as they all felt connected with a world they did not know. It was a miracle. They all turned to look into each other's eyes.

Zapata was speaking now. "You see what this means?" he cried. "There is a leader, Madera from the north, who has a plan for Mexico. We will hear about it. We have a voice now. Those of you who cannot read will meet at the cabin of Tepepe and line up, and we will read this paper to you all day and all night. You will hear it."

A shout went up. "Viva, viva—what?"

Zapata raised his hat. "Viva Tierra y Libertad!"

The Rurales began to circle them as they all shouted, "Long Live Land and Liberty!"

"Begin!" they all shouted. "Let us begin!"

A woman called, "The market tomorrow at Cuautla, the market. Let everyone at the market hear what is in this paper," she shouted.

"How about our animals? How will we free our animals before it is too late? My Cleofas. My goats." They were all pressing upon Zapata and pointing to the meadow. They were telling him about the machine guns again, and there was Anaya closest to him and pointing and telling him, and then holding up one hand, and his thumb, showing Zapata there were six—six machine guns armed by six soldiers—pointed at them.

This seemed to go through Zapata like a rod of lightning. Anger seemed to flash from him. Timoteo heard him say, "Six!" and he pointed to Penales, Orozco, Fuentes, his brother Eufemio, Pablo, and himself, exactly six. They mounted their horses and took their quirts from the horns. What were they going to do?

"Keep under cover. Keep in your houses. All your animals will come home," Montana shouted.

The women turned and ran like a covey of startled birds. The Zócalo was empty. Timoteo and Alfredo and Anaya ran as fast as they could toward the meadow, following the horses. The Rurales were too surprised, wheeling, turning, 'til all followed toward the meadow. Others were running to release the animals.

Timoteo was running with them. He did not feel like himself. He found himself shouting without knowing it. And running until his heart beat like a drum and passing Tepepe who knew how to run a long way through the mountains at a dog trot. Down the road, they saw the ancient pasture and the fence surrounding it, a new kind of fence called barbed wire which they had never seen before, made in Norteamerica, with little barbs on it that cut the skins of animals and caught in the clothes of men and held you. They saw the six machine guns facing the west, where the sun was going down, so it shone in the eyes of the soldiers, who kept the guns pointed at the horsemen, who seemed to be riding straight towards them. They must have thought this was suicidal, for they simply tried to see through the sun in their eyes and did not shoot. The Rurales had been taken by surprise and had not gotten there yet.

Zapata and the other five simply hacked the barbed fence apart with their machetes and now rode away from Timoteo.

Timoteo hardly believed what Zapata was doing. It was too impossible. He saw the six men burst their horses into speed, ride straight towards the pointed machine guns, startling the soldiers. The coyote yells of Zapata and his men rattled the soldiers so they felt, rather than saw, their machine guns lassoed by the approaching men on horseback, actually saw the machine guns start to run after the whooping men who now had turned tail and were flying over the field, each with a machine gun following him. Yes, they had lassoed the machine guns right out of the hands of their gunners, who now stood comical and helpless in the evening sun, some with their hands out in protest, or just as they had them on the guns, ready to fire.

The horsemen went bouncing down the road, the people now screaming, the funny machine guns rattling and leaping like a new kind of colt after them, scattering parts, which someone ran out to pick up. It occurred to everyone that a machine gun was a good thing to have if you could learn how to work it, firing over and over without stopping, an invention of the norteamericanos. It could kill many men while you were just reloading the old hunting guns.

Now that the villagers had the machine guns, the Rurales bolted in fear ahead of them and into the hacienda. The women now all ran screaming, out of the houses, from the river, from everywhere, shouting, running towards the jail. The doors were opening, and all the cattle were being driven out, everyone calling, laughing, for now Zapata and his men set up the six machine guns on the Zócalo, pointing at the prison. The animals came running out, making much comment also about their freedom, and everyone running to embrace, to greet their own animals.

Timoteo saw Cleofas and his own mother running to her and feeling her sides, still with the calf, crying and hugging her and pressing her head against her breast. Timoteo ran and embraced his mother and stroked the soft nose of Cleofas. He was shouting, crying himself.

"Mama! Mama! You should have seen them lassoing the machine guns!"

"Lassoing the machine guns?" she cried.

"Yes, like the pass of death, riding straight at them, lassoing them like bulls, and pulling them right out of the hands of the soldiers!"

Everyone was telling this to everyone else.

Now they saw six machine guns guarding them, and Zapata helping his own mother get her goats and drive them home.

It was a new day for them all.

Chapter 6

That afternoon, long lines passed by Montana on the side of the Zócalo and the Ink Pot on the other as they read from the mysterious newspaper *Regeneración* from St. Louieeeee on the Mississippi River. Another line went through Tepepe's hut, and a young teacher from Cuernavaca read to them. Timoteo brought ollas of water for their parched throats. He listened to what they read and wondered more and more at the magic of the word and how it was printed so it could go all over Mexico, by train, burro, horseback, and be found in the boot of such companions as Pablo from the little village of Anenecuilco, and give people such information and courage and light up their faces. He saw it happen all afternoon.

Once he stood beside the Ink Pot and tried to follow the strange movement of the letters. He saw how the words were separated and came together again. He listened with astonishment. Nothing is left for the man who tills the soil. Bitter poverty for the Indio. A one-crop country is death to the people. Who can live on sugar cane? Everything is in the hands of the foreign invader, nothing in our hands. We must claim the lands of our fathers. And then the stories about the miners of Sonora, the weavers of Puebla, the farmers of Jalisco, the fishermen of Vera Cruz, and the silver miners of San Luis Potosi—places he had never heard of but were part of Mexico. Sometimes a question was asked: "Where is Sonora?" The Ink Pot would draw a map with a stick, showing it was far north, next to California.

"How ignorant we are," Anaya said. "We know nothing."

"I did not know of our ignorance before," Alfredo said. "They have kept us ignorant on purpose. You can see how our ignorance is for their good only."

"I think the first thing we have to do is get rid of our terrible ignorance," Timoteo said. They all nodded together solemnly and sadly.

One line would listen and then move away and tell the others, and another line would move up and Montana and the Ink Pot would tell it all over again. Montana said to them, "You see ignorance is part of being governed by someone beside yourselves. It is a truth that in North America when they were governed by a foreign country, by England, they also could not read or count. Now you see they had a revolution and got free of the foreign country, and now they have much reading and huge newspapers printed every day and read by everyone."

"Everyone can do the reading?"

"Yes, why not? It is part of liberty that the poorest should be able to have knowledge—not live in blindness."

"We didn't know this," they said, moving away for the next group, shaking their heads in wonderment as the Ink Pot told them that the printing was not made by a man for each paper, but that a type was set up, and then dipped in ink, and from this thousands of papers were printed over and over from that one model. It was amazing.

The boys hated to leave. The reading went on far into the night until Montana and the Ink Pot were hoarse and a teacher came from Cuautla and many walked into the village, having heard of this wonderful news and of the lassoing of the guns. By evening it looked like a fiesta, and people were examining the guns which were guarded by the committee.

The soldiers were inside the hacienda, very quiet now the guns were pointed at them.

When the sun went down that day, everyone in Anenecuilco felt like a different person, in a different village. Nobody wanted to leave and go back to their homes, but they all planned to take their produce to Cuautla market on the next day, and it too would be a different day for they would now be famous for their daring deeds and honored among their fellows. Besides, it was planned that the Ink Pot and Montana had printed a leaflet that would be put into every boot and pannier and hidden under fishes and thrust into the baskets of vegetables.

Alfredo, Anaya, and Timoteo were both called into the committee headquarters, and each was to take a certain part of the market with the leaflet wrapped in cheese, in petates, in baskets of onions, and they were to see that every village got some of them, put in the hands of those who could read, or taken to the village councils.

Timoteo decided not to tell his mother of his important assignment until she saw how great he was doing it and was proud of him. He was not sure of the danger in it. Perhaps if something happened there would be much danger. He could not tell. But he felt an excitement he had never felt before, just because he could not tell the dangers involved or what would come of it all.

He sneaked up the hill thinking his mother would be angry. It was late and she would have the care of all the animals. But she was standing in the sun at the top of the hill smiling, and beside her lay Cleofus licking a bright copper calf whose pelt shone in the sunlight, and its face was marked with a white perfect star. It was still wet and glistening. Timoteo gave a cry and caressed Cleofus. "You see, mama, she waited for you to help her. You see she did."

"O a beautiful calf with a star, a sacred star, see how perfect a face. A little she-cow who will give milk," she looked at Timoteo. "Well, my little bull calf looks very dusty and tired. Timoteo, dear one, come and wash. Your tortillas are ready with some of the molé to take to market on them for a treat. And brush down your hair."

He looked at his father's quirt and hat and gun on the wall and he said, "Not forever on your knees."

"What did you say? Oh if your father were here, he would tell me everything how it happened all afternoon. What did the paper say? He would tell me. I didn't get to hear. I heard Cleofus crying for me."

Timoteo could remember his father's silent face and his mother raging at him. So he tried now to wear his father's face. But it made him feel like laughing. Looking severely from under his brows, he saw that she had prepared all the things to take to the market. They were wrapped in cloths and neatly stacked by the door to load on the burro, in the morning, so they would get an early start. He saw the big pot of molé tied up in a white cloth, and the plants she sold, and the ripened cheeses also wrapped like gifts in snow-white cloths.

He really felt full of all the things he had heard from the paper about the miners, weavers, farmers, and most of all what had happened to the guns.

"I can tell, my little son, you are trying to keep a secret from me, but your eyes are not yet like those of your father, and his gun is not yet yours, nor his hat nor his quirt he could wrap around an enemy, neat as a noose."

"This afternoon they took the six machine guns and all the ammunition which the soldiers had run away and left. They packed them on burros, and they are safe in the hills. We have now six machine guns."

"Oh, I am afraid of those guns."

"Be less afraid," he said wisely, "when they are in our hands pointed in the direction of the enemy, and not at us."

"And what else?" she said, sitting beside him. "What else happened? Tell me everything!"

"Tomorrow you will know," he said. "I have been honored."

"And what else?" she urged. "What else?" He wouldn't tell her the big thing for fear she would worry and because it was his first assignment in the world, along with the men, and carried great responsibility. When they got to the market, she would see what it was and be proud. But he told her about the newspaper, and she was astonished. "It seems that the people in our whole country, of many languages, that they all suffer as we suffer and that they are all planning to rise together."

"Rise together?" she said with fear. "A war?"

"I don't know now," he said. "Nobody seems to know. Maybe by the vote. If our votes were truly counted, we could put Madera—he is the new man—in as president of the republic, without bloodshed."

"If they were truly counted," she said. "That is impossible."

"Montana and Zapata think we should do everything before we arm, that we should see if we have the vote as it is said we have by the Constitution."

"That seems good," she said. "Do everything before the firing, and the blood cannot be on the hands of the people."

"Viva, Mama," Timoteo cried, wiping the brown molé off his chin. "You could be a politico!"

"I always told your father that. But a woman!"

"Yes, the paper tells all about the parts of the country, and, Mama, it tells about us."

"Us?"

"Yes, even about Cleofus."

"Cleofus? Don't make a joke, my little son."

"Well, it doesn't know her name, but it tells about our animal, our country. A writer sent it in to the paper some way, and then someone—they have something, Zapata says, a type—and they put it in this type and then from it they can print many papers and send them around the country so that people all know what other people are doing."

She was utterly overcome by this. "More! More!" she cried.

"I have to eat my meal in peace," he said like his father.

"Just like your father," she cried. "I rejoice, my son, with your happiness and cry with your sorrows. Do you think I will run out and tell all the gossips what you tell me?" He could not say that he thought she would.

"Well now, Mamacita, the problem is to get everyone to know what is in this paper, to go all over Morelos, appear at fairs, and markets, and church, and fiestas and tell the people. Every single person, man, woman and child has this to do. Tomorrow as you sell your molés, you must tell this as best you can to the people."

"Tell them what? What, my son?"

"Well, the main thing that others are feeling the same as we feel. That we are all hungry, our land has been stolen, our vote has been stolen, and we are going to get up off our knees."

"Off our knees?"

"And that all the people are going to demand their land back."

"Demand. Demand," she said slowly, "then you will have to fight."

"Yes, we will have to fight."

As if to change the subject, she said, "We will have to start early. I saw a storm lizard at noon."

"Now, mama, that's a superstition."

"Now my son is giving me an education when I have lived five times as long."

"You are ignorant, Mama. I am ignorant. They have kept us in ignorance, as well as keeping our land. We do not even know what takes place in the state next to ours or even in the village."

"I hear enough that is going on in the world. Poor people had better just tend to their milpas."

"And have them taken away from them. What milpas do we have to tend?"

"You are right, my son. I am ignorant. I want you to learn. Will knowledge be part of our new freedom?"

"Yes," he said, "I think freedom gives knowledge, or at least the chance. I think so. I do not know what freedom is, Mamacita."

"We must sleep, she said. "We will look into freedom in the morning."

He felt he had just fallen asleep when he heard his mama crying. "Look, the first light, the primera cock is crowing. No matter what happens, we can keep decent. Here are your clean calzones." They were whiter than snow, beaten by her hands on the rocks of the river and laid in the sun. "When my girls were here and your papa, everyone said no one had whiter clothes when we went to market, and what a sight we were when we had so much to take. I had to kill the last old hen for the pollo. Now we won't have any eggs. But I have a wise son, and what more can a woman want?"

"Don't make fun, Mama. I will be wise."

"Of course you will, my son," she said, pressing his black head to her. And nobody being around, he let himself go, encircled her with his arms, and let his head press into the good odor of herb and corn that always came from her. "Here," she said, "I think you should carry your father's quirt this day. May you be able to use it with the command he had."

He took the quirt so firmly braided, the handle still with memory of his father's hand.

The big hat and the gun still hung there as he looked back going to get the burro for his mama to ride.

He started to go back to tell Inocencio goodbye, but then he didn't. With his father's quirt in his hand, he felt he was too old.

When he had put his mother in the saddle and tied the panniers of cheese on the side, the little white burro knew they were going to market and stepped out very nicely. And he, walking alongside with his father's quirt, and greeting everyone. You couldn't help seeing it was another day, not a day like the day before, or the day before that, or any day before the day where they had lassoed the machine guns. And now it had gone all over the state of Morelos, and people were talking and would greet them in the market with new eyes. It seemed to them all as they passed that the big-walled hacienda was very quiet, the big gates closed, not a soul in sight— cooking up an answer—they laughed behind their hands. Everyone had a secret little smile, and those who hadn't heard were telling the others how, yes, they had ridden straight into the snouts of the machine guns, lassoed them with their quirts, and ridden off with them big as you please. There was more talk than usual. Of late, there had been silence and grim endurance and just going to market with the little that you had, to bargain and trade for the little you could afford.

Every village had their market day, and some vendors made them all mostly by walking with their packs on their backs. It was their meeting place as well, where all the news was pooled and the gossip exchanged, and families met who had been separated from their village by work or marriage.

They met folks from the villages south bringing plums from Tlayacapan, peaches from Totolapan, and limes from Tlalnepantla. From Jonacatepec oranges, from Yautepec bananas and guavas. Pack trains came from as far as Toluca over the Sierras where the weaving was of the best, and you used to get your winter serapes when the crops were good. There were black and tan potters and basket makers and fellows with copper faces from the south selling petates, pottery peddlars from Cuernavaca, rope makers from Tepoztlán, sooty-faced carabineros from the Sierras of the Ajuscos, where they spent the days in the forests making coke. There would be acrobats and gypsies, trains of shaggy mountain ponies carrying mariachi players. There one would see many different faces, pure patterns of the ancient races from which they had come, as if time were but a day. You would also hear many languages spoken that were so old and had no written alphabet and were passed down from father to son. The women rode side by side or walked under their rebozos telling who had died, who had been born.

They walked between fields of cane and steaming rice paddies, always in the sight of the big snow-covered volcano rising splendid in the day's light. There were singers and guitar players and groups of merry girls carrying their white-wrapped cheeses and singing lustily. There came Tepepe taking a goat to market to sell, with his trumpet wrapped and hugged close to him. "What are you going to blow today, Tepepe," they called to him, "a call to battle?" He grinned and went on with his goat.

It was still in the ripe morning when they entered Cuautla. Just as they crossed the river, there was the sound of hooves behind them, and Zapata and his brother and four others galloped into the city. When they came into the market with its canopies stretching down the side streets and the women already sitting before their bright wares, they were greeted by his father's friends smiling. He was proud of his mamacita sitting in her full skirts, excited, and her black braids switching behind her, like he used to see her when his father was alive and his sisters did the housework and they had rich corn lands to live from.

He went behind the weavers' store where he had been told to go. There he was given a sheepskin to try and sell as a blind man, and the leaflets run off by Montana the night before to distribute to those who could read. He stuck them up his white blouse and returned and helped his mother set up her little table, and thinking he must get her a little canopy to keep the sun off her like the others had. And then he slid away while she wasn't looking, but that was nothing unusual.

At first he sidled up to the friends of his father, men that he knew. The old sires looked down at him through their whiskers as he handed them the leaflet and told them that, if they couldn't read, they would get someone to read it to the whole village. He stood up to them, and they were astonished when he told them about the rest of the country. "How can we be together?" they would ask. "We are together in our suffering, in our loss of land. That brings us together. No, Señor, if you will take some of these, return to your village and keep talking, go out at night and visit every shepherd in your barrio. If everyone does this, we will soon be of one mind. Then one day Zapata or Maestro Montana will come and speak. We have men of great learning with us now, a man named Madera."

"Now tell it to me again, muchacho," they would say, leaning down to listen. "The young now must teach the old. Where did you learn to read?"

Timoteo would not say he could or could not read. He would hold the paper up as Zapata did and say what was in it. "It says here that in Vera Cruz," he would say, and then as if reading he would tell the story as he had heard it, "it says the girls went out of the factory because they didn't get enough to live on and the soldiers shot at them."

"Shot at them?"

"Yes. You see, here it tells about them. Otherwise you would not hear about them or they about us."

"We are truly men in darkness," the old men said, looking sad and old, but strong under their sombreros.

"Yes," Timoteo said sadly, and he was never to forget it, "men in darkness. We must come out of the darkness together."

It was a miracle how just the information about each other was so freeing. This, Timoteo thought, is what is meant by ignorance.

He had never talked so much in his life. His mouth got dry as in a drouth. He saw Zapata once talking to a group that surrounded him, but when the police appeared there was nobody there but an old shoe mender sitting and hammering at a piece of leather. He would see such groups and then, before his eyes, so he would think maybe he had not seen them, they would melt away. He went to talk to the women. Sometimes they were more difficult and sometimes they seemed to have been waiting all their lives just to hear what he had to tell them. They would take his little paper and carefully fold it and put it in their pockets or safely under the tortillas.

He felt very hungry and feared his mother may have sold all her chicken with molé. Almost all the women gave him a bit of fruit. He found her looking as flushed as himself. She leaned over like a conspirator. "I have been telling them everything you told me," she said. "I have been telling them too about Hidalgo and Juárez and even Señor your father told me about."

"Bravo, Mamacita. I am starving."

"Have you a fever, my son? Your face is red. Let me see if you have a fever."

"No, Mamacita, I have no fever. I never felt better in my life."

"Shhhhh," she said. It was the soldiers marching by, and for the first time in his life he felt no fear of them or anything.

"You never felt better," she said after they had passed.

"Never better."

She smiled. "There is something about the market, about the people, I have never seen before, as if something was changing, turning."

"Yes, that is it. We can look through a door and see a future. Before it was only a blank adobe wall."

"I am afraid, son."

"Don't be afraid of anything, Zapata says, but to live on your knees forever as a slave."

"Oh, my son, you are going to be a man with words."

"Words," Timoteo said, "I have seen this day are weapons. Maybe they are as good as guns." She shivered and they began to pack their things for the return journey. Everyone went slowly home, enjoying the thought of their bargains, of their sales, and on this day something more. They had heard words they never heard before. These words had been bored into them as you place a seed deep in a furrow when you plant corn. These words would sprout in the heat of the coming days, and they looked at their land now as if it might rise as some beloved dead person and return to them.

Timoteo and his mother and Tepepe, his mother riding the burro, went to the road to Anenecuilco. The great light, like blood, ran down the sides of the Popocatétl. Its whole base was in a blue haze that dreamlike spread down into the valleys of their conquered land. The land lay before them shackled, but all saw how they could cut the cords of its binding.

Slowly, half in sleep, they jogged in their two-wheeled carts or on their little horses or donkeys, babies wrapped in their mothers' rebozos, children sleeping on their fathers' shoulders or in the hay and empty pots. It was quiet. Sometimes a child whimpered, an animal cried out, but it was the land that rose like a chained woman, crying out to them in her blue rebozo, holding out her captive arms to them. Timoteo walked behind the black braids of his mother, who sat silent. He saw her looking through the gloom at the milpas of her grandfather which lay to the left towards the mountains. He knew she was saying the exact dimension to herself, how it lay, and how it was recorded in the ancient records. And she knew the communal land which belonged to the village and was cultivated by all. If you did not use the land and use it properly, it returned to the village holdings. All land was for the good and security of all the people.

He began to estimate how many cargos of corn it would take to reseed his great grandfather's land, and then he knew that the people on the road were silent because they were all again free men, planting and reaping their land, eating their tortillas in plenty and in peace, caring for each other in the old and ancient ways.

He grasped the handle of his father's quirt as if it might be his father's hand.

Chapter 7

The little Ink Pot had no trouble any more teaching the alphabet to two classes a day. Timoteo, Alfredo and Anya went every evening after the cows were milked and bedded down and drew A B C in the dust and learned to spell Z a p a t a and their own names, and finally could write what is called a sentence: We want our land. That was a proud day. They learned to spell this out from the leaflet they were going to take to Jojutia, and in big black letters it said at the top WE WANT OUR LAND. And the other one said VOTE FOR LEVYA. The three of them could swim through the villages like eels and in no time distribute a whole basket of leaflets hidden under a load of melons or squash blossoms or tortillas. The villagers got to know them and held out their hands for the leaflets which they would quickly fold into their shirts or slip into a package of fish or rice.

It was never the same for the two boys. The people of Anenecuilco had changed. Every man, woman and child had changed in one way or another according to his nature. By this time, the farthest shepherds high in the hills had heard of all that had happened. The committee had opened an office, even in Cuautla, where their candidate was there for anyone to talk to and see—a man named Levya, a lawyer who had the boldness, with the support, as he said, of the committee and the people, to run for President against Díaz. Díaz himself came down to see what was up. There they made themselves a little newspaper. People came in and out all day and all night, sleeping on the floor, taking the latest news out to the readers known in every village, where it was passed on to the people.

All we are asking for is the vote, the leaflets said. Vote your lands back peacefully. Díaz says we have a democracy. Find out by voting. Zapata appeared everywhere, and Montana and the Magnani brothers and the Ink Pot and other teachers and lawyers joined them, some from the city, coming down to help. Zapata would appear in a field, at the markets, a circus, a rodeo, a bullfight, stand in his stirrups and shout. Vote for your own candidate, Levya. Vote for your state, Morelos. Vote for your family. And he would be off before the police would appear. The government now openly pursued him.

Zapata would say—after the vote—if we are tricked again, then we will fight. It would go out into the fields, in the cantinas, in the market place. We will fight.

At Anenecuilco, strange things were heard. The women washing would ask each other: Did you hear it last night? Hear what? A strange sound like the last horn of Cuatéhmoc, the last defender of our land. Maybe he has returned to help us now. I heard it, another would say, as if the mountain opened, and, when I looked out, I saw no light, only the stars. Maybe it is Cuatéhmoc, the sierras open for him, and he comes in his feathers to fight Díaz as he fought Cortez. Some said maybe it is Hidalgo and the grita, the cry for freedom. Maybe it is Juárez marching with Abraham Lincoln to save México. Timoteo said nothing, not even when his mama said to him, "Today when I was washing in the stream, there was a sound coming from the hills where you and Tepepe have been with the animals."

"Sound of what, Mama?" Timoteo said innocently.

"Well, no one could quite say, like a call to battle. It might be called that, all the women heard it."

"Was it a good sound, Mama?"

"Oh, a very good sound, clear like a call from your heart."

"Then there is no worry if it was good. No need to get the curandero to consult the owls, Mama. Let it be a good sound."

As the elections came nearer, the Rurales and the army began to march on the roads and to appear suddenly at the fairs, although this was very hard now, because every child, every bird, every burro gave them warning. The whole state of Morelos was roused, ready to vote, to test the democracy of their country.

One day, Tepepe had said to Timoteo, "I am an old man. A wind might blow me away or I might blow clear through the bugle and disappear in a note. There is nobody to leave my bugle to. My sons have all gone to the north, refusing to be slaves or work for the low wages here. I do not read and perhaps they do not write, so I never hear if they still live. Timoteo, you are my son and I must leave you my bugle, and

I must also leave you my skill." So he handed Timoteo the shining simple bugle that got very hot in the sun and began the first lesson. "Now, as you know, a bugle takes a man to blow it. It has no frets for the tones, put your fingers on to sound the notes. A man must blow the notes right out of his own body, right out of the earth. You must be like the god of wind, and it must be controlled right in your own lungs. You must come right into the bugle. You see how it is."

He taught him to practice and get a tough mouth, for the lips have to change form, and you have to form the tones before they come out. "You have a good ear, a pure ear, otherwise you could not make the sounds like the instruments of today. They make the tone for you, but the best flute is still the one where you change the wind." So Timoteo took the trumpet that had come down from father to son for many generations and bore the dents of the bullets of Puebla where his own grandfather had been killed in the fight against the French. He raised the horn hot from the sun, planted his feet firmly on the earth, took in the wind on a great gulp of summer flowers, stored it in the bottom of his ribs, made a big fist of it, changed it to his own air, felt it come to his mouth, changed it there, mouthed it and pitched it out into a terrible blast that made Inocencio jump three feet into the air and set the animals humming and the jackass to braying.

"Come here!" Tepepe shouted, throwing himself on the ground by the burro. "Look at the bellows here. See how his tone comes from his back legs, from his hoof as if from a kick. He pulls the sound of the ground, comes like a quirt up his back legs. Look, he brings it up into his bellows." He was pointing at the tense grey loins as the burrow bellowed his awesome "he haww he haww," as if the sound was blown up from this little thin rear end, gathered together as a fearful kick and passed up to blast against his bare teeth, thrown like a ball of sound from the belly, in a fierce hurricane into his blown-out nostrils, "No, come in front," Tepepe darted on the ground, and Timoteo looked up into the dilated nose holes. "That's his trumpet. He makes it out of his nose. Look at his lips curled back for a mouthpiece. Here it comes, hades wind of a tornado blasted up in his own trumpet, up the throat and through the curled black lips and maybe his teeth make the change in sound. I don't know—peewee yeeeyeeeee—you could hear it for a long ways."

Pretty soon he could hold the air like a fist in his heart and lungs and feel it quiver on his lips like birds pecking him. Then the air would vibrate the metal. He could feel it like a living bird in his hands, and then easy and long came the pure pure note of C as if it rode upon the air, and he let it go longer and longer until the donkey's ears twitched and Inocencio came and sat with his bare feet to feel the vibration go back into the ground.

When the note was good, Tepepe would do a weird old dance. "Just a little quaver is alright," he would say, "to make you quake, to plead with you a little. These sounds enter the air and enter the heart. That's why you have to have a bugler, no matter what is happening, a bullfight, a battle, a Diana, a wedding, a funeral. This sound goes right through the body. The trumpet is made like the body. It leaps and plunges through a person. Men whose bowels have shrunk in terror in a battle must feel courage from the pure notes that come from you, feel like they spring up with thousands of others and that they cannot lose. When they are losing, this is the most important time for the bugler, remember that. And when they are winning, the bugler announces it to all, as he does in the Diana when the man and bull have done well together. For all this, you must be pure and understand all the history behind a note.

"I am a pure follower of Zapata," Timoteo said proudly, and I will blow good.

"Good. Now see if you can go from C to E *mmmmmmmm* and *mmmmmmmm*."

Timoteo felt his ears itch and all his being searching, rising to the note, and there golden it came out of his flared mouth, and there it was, the note E pure and true. Then Tepepe would really go mad and shout and hum up to G, waving like a conductor, shouting, "Hold it, hold it, that's it!"

Inocencio began to make strange noises and blow out his whole body so they had to laugh.

"Once you get it true, you never forget it. I can hear my bugling at the battle of Puebla like it as yesterday. I was very good. I was young and true and every man who heard it remembers it and hears it again at night in his sleep."

"I believe it," Timoteo said. "Now I am a trumpeter for freedom."

"Freedom is a big word and should be used well and sparingly."

"I believe it." So Timoteo began to learn.

Timoteo's mother became frightened, for now Timoteo was gone most of the time. Tepepe had the flocks of all the others who went to protect Zapata. Zapata came to see her and told her, "You were my mother's best friend. Don't think I have forgotten. I would have nothing happen to Timoteo here, but we need him. He is quick and has much good in him. The young boys can do much for us. They can go where we cannot go, disappear quickly, deliver messages." He and Timoteo both kissed her and she said, "I am not of the ignorant. I had a father died for liberty and a husband, and now, if I have a son also, I will know how to act."

"Look after Inocencio," Timoteo said, "Just give him a fat fly a day or let him out and he will catch his own."

"Don't worry, Timoteo, I will catch flies for him. Never fear."

Zapata laughed, and, as they went, he said, "Remember this now. This is how it will be at Jojutla, where we are now going. You will get rid of your papers, and then—in case nothing happens, or in case something does—you will run to the wall of this number and a woman will expect you as you jump over the wall, then..." And he told him every detail and how they would all then meet on a split second, at the big hog plum tree and ride double to the cactus hills.

Zapata took him to a two-wheeled car in Cuautla driven by a man he had never seen before, Luis by name, covered and concealed behind large black mustachios and a hat drawn down over shaggy black hair. The leaflets were packed in some large cooking pots full of hay, and one was empty so that he could hide in if it was necessary. They jogged on in the heat to Jojutla, which was a large town separated from Cuautla by a sugar cane valley and then some barren cactus hills, and then what looked like a camp of sugar cane mill workers. But it turned out to be the committee for Levya, who had been there two days, some of them working in the cane fields as a cover. They had organized the whole thing and the getaway. There were lookouts everywhere, on every street.

As they approached Jojutla, the road was crowded with people. Timoteo had to take off his serape and one shirt, it was so hot. You had to dress so you could take off three shirts at noon and put them all on at night when the cold winds came down from the mountains.

They drove in with all the other peddlers, and the barter and purchase, worship and frolic had begun. The market was crowded. His pockets and pants were already filled with leaflets. He left Luis in the market where he could return for more, cautioning him not to sell the big pots that contained the leaflets. Everybody now expected leaflets and information. It was quite different than it had been at first. You needed to persuade no one. Eagerly they tucked the leaflet inside their palm, quickly into a pocket or inside their shirts or in a pot, or under a fish's head, or into a rope blanket. Some recognized him and held out hands for them. He would skitter through the crowd, spotting the shady-looking characters or secret service men or informers. Sometimes a woman would push him behind her skirts until the local gendarme had passed. Once he was lifted bodily and put into a huge basket until the policeman had gone on.

People gave him delicious tortillas and fruits of every kind in season. It gave him much pleasure to think of how the little leaflets would be taken out in far places and corners of the state of Morelos, carefully unfolded, smoothed out, and leaning over in acote flares and candle light. They would slowly try to read what was there. Now he knew how his father had felt all his life, belonging to some secret society that fought the invader, as his father always called the Spanish. How his father felt that winter day, walking with the committee to Cuernavaca to protest the seizure of their last land. How much courage it takes to speak out and now he had it. He was doing it. He felt surrounded as in a garden with the secret love of people he had never seen before.

An old man put his hand on Timoteo's shoulder, frightening him. "Timoteo, I knew your father. Be proud."

"I am proud," he said, and darted off to his post near the fountain, where he washed the dust off his face and hands and wet his hair. He had never been to a speech-making like this, and he wondered how they would bring it off before the Rurales or the local police could come down on them. He saw across the street at the far side of the plaza where he was supposed to run. Yes, it was the right number, and he could make it across in nothing flat if he had to. Suppose, though, someone was shooting at him. Could he make it? Anything was possible now. He thought he was taller, too, a better target the taller you get. Well, he would make it to the first wall and hoped the women would be there, maybe with some cheese and tacos.

Suddenly the plaza began to fill as if water was running in it from all the spokes of streets that ran into it and carried with them on his horse, but slowly carried as if upon a stream of moving water. He saw Zapata. Behind him was Eufemio, and far back he could see the other horsemen. When he got to the center, he held up his hand and there was silence. And there he was in the midst of the mass of people who seem to hold him up as well as protect him. He called out, "Campesinos, Señors, Señoras. " Timoteo stood tip-toe on the fountain rim. Zapata had a great voice. "You received a paper which will tell you to vote for our candidate Levya. You will vote for the first time in your life, some of you. We will see if what they say is true, that we are citizens, that our country belongs to us, that we can vote in our man. If this is not true, then we will know what to do."

Someone started a viva, but Zapata held up his hand. There was no sight of the enemy to Timoteo, and the faces of his people spread before him like flowers in a meadow.

"We must rise from our forlornness and misery. We must come face to face with our enemies. You feel you are ignorant, men and women in darkness, forsaken by all. I propose that you, the humildes, if you do not elect your man, create an army of the people on their feet fighting. Now, we all know to get a horse to do something that is hard for him or almost impossible, you have to put spirit into him. Alone he is afraid. If you want him to go over a bluff or make a dangerous jump, you don't put it to him cold. You warm him up. You give him your spirit, make him feel that you know he can do it. Now it's the same with us. We are faced with a task that is very hard.

We have got to make each other feel we can win. Everything is in the spirit, whether horse or man. There is nothing a man can't do, nothing a people can't do if they get the spirit together. We are braver. We can do more than we know. That's what we must all do. We must make each other believe every minute that we can do it. The fire that burns in every man and woman will burn. Suffering and anger will give us strength. Silent and forgotten, we will speak."

There was a cry outside the mass of people, a stir. Their massive intensity broke, they moved apart. Timoteo did not know how it all happened. It was so well organized and done so quickly. Zapata said quickly, "I am going now. Remember and repeat everything you have heard here. And if Díaz does not honor our vote, then you know what to do. Every man a general, and every hunting gun down from the wall."

Timoteo began to run before he knew it. He saw the people open up, press close, allow the horsemen through. Then he saw that the Rurales were trying to push towards the eddying horsemen. But the people did not lift a hand against them. They simply stood solid so they could not move and took the lashes of the quirts across their backs. They eddied around Zapata and his men, and they were pushed in the clear. And, as he ran, he heard the sound of their horses' hooves galloping out of town. He made the wall, and sure enough there was a woman in a black rebozo. She said, "My little son, did they get away?" And she hung from his should a bag of tortillas and boosted him sharply over the farthest wall so that he flew over and landed on his knees. It was dead silent there, and he took to his feet through the old ruins of the Aztec walls, entered a broken entrance where grass grew from the black stone, climbed a grassy mounded pyramid. Down the other side was the meadow just as Zapata had said, and it was quiet and clear. He could just see the church spires of Jojutla, and there not a half mile before him, he saw the hog plum tree spreading its great branches like elephant trunks. Almost at the same time, the horses thundered up. To his delight, it was Emiliano, who leaned down and scooped him up. With lightness and pride, he straddled the powerful horse, and they were all galloping toward the sierras where Zapata knew every hill and hut, every shepherd and milpas, every path of the ancients which led across the volcano and down into the city of Mexico, which later he was to take a whole army through, over the pass and into the city. Timoteo could hear his words, the abandoned and forlorn, the silent and the harassed.

It was a long ride in the night, and nobody was following them. But he was happy riding with the great Zapata, whom he now saw growing out of his old husk. Like Montana said, it was the people who made you great, and Zapata was becoming great from the people. Why, even he himself, a boy, was filled with the strength of the people beyond himself. He did not know that he almost slept and was held in front with the gentle arm of Zapata until he was gently slid off at his mother's door in the deep of the night. She stood with a little light. "You are safe." "Yes," Zapata said, "a wonderful meeting." Timoteo said, "Have we won?" Zapata laughed. "Day after tomorrow, the elections, then we will know." "Alight," the mother said, "and have something hot." "Gracias," Zapata said, "but I am going to sleep back in the hills. They are not going to pick me off before the elections. I am going to count the votes. Buenas noches, mother." And he plunged up the hill instead of down, away from the village to the hills, where his sleep would be watched.

Timoteo allowed his mother to draw him into the smoky, sweet-smelling house and down to a hot bowl of beans, and he ran to the door with the sack of tortillas he had meant to give. "Zapata, Emiliano, Zapata," he called. His mother drew him back gently and to sleep.

Chapter 8

The three boys had run like rabbits from Jojutla through the Wolf's Canyon. They had met no one and, now laughing, threw themselves panting in the bushes away from the road.

"Did you get rid of yours?" Timoteo asked, opening his jacket where he kept the leaflets.

Alfredo and Anaya both opened their jackets and showed only themselves inside. "All gone," they crowed, "every one!"

They had gone through Jojutla like three smokes, sticking the Levya leaflets into every pocket and burro's ear. The people had come past them with their hands outstretched behind them and, quick as a flash, they could put the leaflets anywhere. It would take a quick eye of the Rurales to catch them. The leaflet said in big letters "VOTE" and then Levya's slogan, "Tierra y Agua! Land and Water!"

But they had gotten bold and did not notice that two horsemen had followed them out of the village. They had an hour's journey back to Cuautla and six miles further to

Anencuilco. Zapata had told them to keep to the ridges and not be out after dark alone.

Alfredo began to draw letters in the dirt with his big toe. "How does the M and N go?" he said, and Timoteo brought his own toe to the soft dirt to show.

Anaya was thinking of something else. "Now I know," he said, and the glow of the last sun shone on his ancient Indian face. "Now I know what Tepepe means when he tells about when they came back from the battles with the French at Puebla. Those battles for their freedom have shone on their faces all these years."

Timoteo said, "My mama said that when she saw my father coming down the road, coming home, that he too shone, and there never was a man to look like him."

Alfredo said laughing, "You both are shining. You look on fire. You are lighted up like firecrackers."

"I have been this way," Timoteo said, "since we got our animals back and Zapata and all of them lassoed the machine guns." And he rolled over hugging himself with joy, and the other two leaned over and touched him, laughing. "Then all was hidden. We didn't dare to speak or sneeze. Now we can be seen and we can see each other!"

"It isn't the sun," Anaya said, "it is the light of freedom. It is passed from one man to another and so it is always lit like a torch."

The boys were silent and the last sun shone on their faces.

"You know what the little school teacher, Montana, says."

"What does he say?"

"Oh, he says many things. He is a teacher. Everything you do now he gives you a lesson from it!"

"Well, there is a lesson to learn. We are like babes just learning to walk."

"And talk."

"And read."

"Think of that," Anaya said.

"Think of what?"

"Think of the village documents that have been saved since the Nahautl tribes crossed the Ajusco Mountains, before the birth of Jesús, and mixed with Mazatepac with Toltecs and Chichimecas who founded the province of Tláhuac, which is now our state of Morelos. We were an agriculture people."

"Listen, do you hear anything?"

Anaya stopped, "I thought I heard horses coming down the road."

"Well, we are not seen here in the bush."

Anaya continued. "We had seed and, above all, cotton. But we left records, documents. Zapata and Montana spent a week in the church choir loft trying to read them, all in Nahautl, when the village turned them over when he became Calpuleque, the jefe of the village. These papers establish all our rights to the land and water. They finally sent Franco with the maps to Tetelcingo where the Nahautl language had been preserved. A priest from the village of Tepoztlán was able to read it. Imagine, those documents kept since before Jesús was born—years before that!"

And Alfredo leaned over whispering, "You know who has them? Franco, and Zapata told him he is not to fight on any front. He is to safeguard these papers with the ancient words and signs upon them. Zapata says these papers contain the reason for our struggles. We will need them when we win. Imagine those papers in all the wars, the Aztecs, the French, the Spanish—and now the haciendados—being kept by the old men, guarded for us."

They all three sat with their knees drawn up—in wonder. Anaya said suddenly, solemnly, "Montana says whoever finds freedom finds his country, but this is my country, slave or free. I intend to be here. I intend to stand up here. When I am dead, I will be in my country, in its earth, in its sweet earth. It is my country!"

Timoteo leaned over and took his hands.

"Listen!" Alfredo said suddenly. "Let's move. Come on! Be careful!" They took a swig out of their water bottle, and then they came out of the barranca looking up and down the now darkening road. "We have waited too long. It is getting dark," Timoteo said.

"Maybe we should not take the road," Anaya said.

"Oh, there is nobody and it is so hard going on the ridges."

"Keep a lookout behind, Anaya," Timoteo said, "and I'll go front."

They had hardly gone a mile when the Rurales' horses plunged down in front of them from the bank. Timoteo, a little in front, broke for the bush and a shot was fired after him. While they were corralling Anaya, Alfredo plunged into the other embankment out of sight. The soldiers fired. They both seemed to pass out of sight instantly, and the mesquite and cacti were thick there. Timoteo tore his pants and the skin of his legs on the thorns, but he burrowed into the thick underbrush. He heard the shot fired at Alfredo, as he heard the voices of the men, swearing at Anaya, angered that the other two got away and the horses were neighing and plunging. They tried to beat the brush, but the thorns tore their uniforms and, swearing, they mounted Anaya behind one of them. Timoteo heard the beat of the hooves of the horses clatter close to him and then fade away down the road as they turned around the canyon.

He waited, trying to hear if Alfredo had escaped the shot. He began to swear at himself. How careless they had gotten, not to scout back and see if they had been followed. And to sit and talk and not hurry before the dark came down. Where was Alfredo? But just then he saw Alfredo's scared face as he crawled to him. Timoteo swore like a shepherd. How could we have let it happen? We are not warriors worthy of even our father's hat. Walking down the roads like patrons when we should have been drifting on the ridges like smoke. He covered his face with his hands.

"Where will they take him?" Alfredo said, wiping the blood off his knees and legs torn by the thorns. "I hear the jail in Cuautla is full."

"Then maybe they will take him home."

"Oh, they'll keep him until after the elections and then they will let him go. They'll let everyone out then."

To punish themselves, they took the back ridges, guided by the last glow from the white beard of Popocatépetl, and it was far into the night when they got back.

There was Tepepe watching for them, and he took hold of Timoteo with his fierce root hands. "Where have you been? They brought Anaya. He is in the jail."

"How can we get him out?" both boys asked.

"Take it slow," Tepepe said. "He will be alright for the night, safer than we are. Zapata is sleeping in the hills well guarded, worn out from riding and speaking in all the villages. Go to your beds. Your mamas are worrying. Go around the square so you won't be recognized."

It was a night full of tensions, even the animals were nervous, baaing and mooing. Nobody slept. Zapata had told everyone to go into their houses and close the doors and not come out 'til morning when the voting started.

Timoteo's mother said, "We are going to have our votes counted tomorrow. We will show Señor Díaz and Señor Jesús that we do not want our land stolen and our animals put in prison."

But Timoteo for the first time cried before his mother. He sat before his papa's picture and he cried. She saw he was not a little boy any more to be comforted, so she sat quietly opposite him and only reached out her hand to cover his.

Timoteo was silent. Something had happened that had never happened to him before. "Anaya was arrested," he cried to his mama. "The soldiers arrested him. We let it happen to him. We got very bold and full of pride and let it happen." And now he cried sitting under his father's picture. He cried without covering his face at all.

He rose in fury and with one gesture took down his father's gun, which he had never touched before.

"No, no!" she cried. "No! It is the vote! Zapata says it is the vote!"

He stood at the door with the gun pointed down at the jail.

My son, my son, she thought. He was going to shoot straight down into the night. He would never even kill a little bird to put in the rice sometime. Do not shoot.

"Yes, Zapata said we would not take up arms until we found out if our vote means anything, if the constitution still lives, if the land is still ours, if liberty means anything."

"Yes, he said that. Come, my son, rest for tomorrow, rest."

He remembered Tepepe saying, "Sleep when you can, get your strength back, take care of your strength."

"Well, we will find out tomorrow," he said. "Yes, mama, I will try to keep my strength, bring it back every night, save it."

He lay on the earth on his grass petate. He saw his mother on her knees grinding corn so she would have plenty of tortillas to feed to the voters, maybe sell some and make a few centavos. He could hear the stone upon the stone and the corn being ground, and he dreamed that he was the corn, being ground fine to feed others who cried "Land and Liberty!"

Chapter 9

Timoteo and his mother were up early, fed the animals, let the frog out of the box for a walk, and went down the path to the village early. The roads were alive with people in their best clothes, greeting each other with a kind of secret joy. The jefe Zapata and his committee were watching the polls. The hacienda guards were also watching, and everyone knew there were machine guns ready to be rolled to the gates.

"It's too quiet," Timoteo said.

His mother said, "For thirty years they have stolen our votes and elected Señor Díaz. They were not going to give up easy." She nudged Timoteo to look at the smokeless stack of the sugar mill. It was closed.

The vote was in by noon, and the vote counting was watched by both sides. There were only the votes of the hacienda for Díaz's man, and Levya got the vote of the three villages. The news went around the hills along the roads—"We won! Levya won!" The people started to gather in the Zócalo. "Wait", the committee sent out word. "No violence. No blood upon our hands. Wait in the hills. Get the women and children back."

But it was too late. Timoteo waited for them to release Anaya. In the after, when the jail doors did not open, the junta went to the iron doors and demanded the freedom of the men. They stood there denied, and then Zapata rose up and shouted in a fearful voice, "Clear the jail! They are not criminals! The criminals are the ones in the big house who have stolen our lands!" The doors were opened and the prisoners poured out. Timoteo cried, "Anaya!" and ran towards him. Anaya seemed blinded by the light and the shouts of the people. The people ran to greet the prisoners, and they all moved to the Zócalo. Then suddenly, Timoteo felt like a fish hooked with a cruel barb, the sound went through his body and he fell flat to the ground, drawing Anaya with him. Timoteo could see women and children falling to the ground, but it never occurred to him that they had been shot. He saw that the walls of the hacienda were studded with the machine guns, and they were firing directly into the people. "Run, Anaya!" Timoteo cried, and took hold of him. They ran toward the river, always their refuge. Timoteo shouted to them all, "Run, run!" They seemed to be huddled together in the Zócalo in the direct fire of the terrible guns.

He thought afterwards that he must have known it when the bullet hit Anaya. He felt him stop, become a terrible weight like stone leaning and falling against him, so he half carried him, his arm under his arm pits and pushing him in front, feeling the bullets at his back. But they seemed suddenly to just fall out of range, and they half fell into the protection of the river, falling down on its banks out of fire. They could hear the sound of the guns' incessant fire, but it seemed like a nightmare one was half sleeping.

It seemed to him afterwards that Anaya was already gone when they half fell into the river and the cold water struck them. He began to tear open his white shirt to find where the bullet had lodged. The blood seemed to be coming out of a sieve. His breast seemed a sieve held in the air and the little holes all red fountains of blood which Timoteo tried to stop with his hands, as if stopping then the precious blood of his friend would change its course. But stopping up the two holes below the heart, the belly spouted holes, and he threw himself upon them crying, although his reason told him that even a surgeon could not have saved him then. He abandoned the body and took his head with the wonderful black hair like a Mayan and his friend's fine face with the big Mayan nose, and now to his amazement the great eyes were open, wide open, and looking at him as his friend did when they searched for knowledge or to find what was true.

They seemed to be open as if they sat amongst the high mountains amidst spring flowers and breezes. They were soft and alive and flashed something to him, seemed to flow over him and say something so clear, so warm. And he bent down, crying, "What, what, Anaya? Tell me, amigo, speak! What? You are going to live. I am going to carry you now to the doctor, Anaya. Live, live, amigo!" But even as he shook the great head and leant over the soft, enormous eyes, the eyes of all his race preserved for a thousand years, the eyes seemed to be growing smaller, disappearing over some horizon. The eyes seemed to become remote as something sinking in water. They became enlarged but covered over with a veil, and Anaya left them, left the young body and the great skull and the heart that yearned for liberty and the brain that yearned for knowledge. He was gone as surely as if he had disappeared in a distance, never to return.

Timoteo did not leave him. He held the friendly head. He felt it get cold, he felt himself get cold. He felt the cold, weeping water of the river they loved, the flesh they loved, and the night of the village all drop into a cold, cold stream. He heard far off the moaning and crying and the oaths of a man who came out into the Zócalo to remove the dead. He lay half in the water as if dead also. Tepepe found him in the night. They had to pry his hands away from the dead body of his friend, and his face from his face, and their common hair matted with blood.

He broke away from Tepepe and ran up the hill to his house, where no light shone, to see if his mother was safe.

She came out of the unlighted door, and she was carrying his father's gun held across her breast, and she had a look he had never seen in her before, and she strode towards him and put the gun in his hands.

Chapter 10

Timoteo all his life was never to forget the sound the next morning of Anaya's old father making the wooden coffin for Anaya's body, the sound of the hammer on wood, the sound of many hammers on coffins were made for the dead.

The village was very dangerous, and the dead lay in the sanctuary of the church. The town was filled with soldiers. Proclamations were put on the walls that the Díaz candidate had won and were mysteriously torn down.

The black-shawled women came and went to the church. The bell tolled. The fields were empty, the mill was closed, and even the servants at the hacienda did not appear for work.

Anaya's body was brought to the church around eleven, and Alfredo and Timoteo were the first to stand guard beside his coffin, one standing on each side with guns nearly as tall as they. Timoteo tried not to look at the sleeping face of his friend. But he kept hearing his words as they squatted in the dirt of Wolf Canyon. Standing there hour after hour, something hardened in him, clenched like a fist. When

Anaya's father touched his shoulder in the afternoon to relieve his watch, he felt that his whole body had become a weapon.

The church was filling. People came and went from every village. Before the altar lay five women, four children, two shepherds and Anaya. People who had hidden in the hills came down at night and slipped into the church to mourn. In the evening, the choir sang. Timoteo and Alfredo stood guard again in the night. The incense was thick, and it seemed some terrible dream, the dead as if witnesses to some hidden violence which lay day and night for centuries beneath their lives, taking their strength, suddenly leaping out, destroying them.

Anaya seemed to be sinking away from them all, and Timoteo in the night tried to memorize his face to be before him always and be given to the eyes of his unborn children.

Zapata came and embraced Timoteo and Alfredo and made a prayer before each one of the dead, and Timoteo saw his jaw tighten and felt he had also made a vow, a promise, to the dead.

When the morning came, the Zócalo was filled with people, and the church was packed, and the village was a solid black mass of mourning and angry people.

Father Hidalgo made a bold sermon, blaming the hacienda for the violence and defending the right of voting under the Constitution. Timoteo carried one end of the coffin, Alfredo opposite him, Anaya's father and uncle carrying the other end, and all the people following them to the cemetery, the chorus of women singing, the weepers, the committee walking together, and Timoteo blew a great salvo on the horn.

Anaya's father, after the priest, spoke about the life of his son and the lives of all of them and how now was the time. They had no choice for all the young men, and he put his arm around Timoteo and Alfredo for the lives of children not yet born. They stood at the brink of a great and terrible revolution in which many would give their lives for land and liberty.

The afternoon turned golden and strange. Timoteo stood beside his comrades and beside his mother, with a new sternness he took from the face of Anaya, which he was never to lose.

It was late evening that the news went around like wildfire that they had arrested Zapata. The government had arrested him, and he was even then in the jail at Cuautla and would on the morrow be taken across Wolf Canyon to Cuernavaca where he would be charged with evading military services.

They couldn't get him with a bullet, everyone said, but with a piece of paper, what cowardice, a legal attack. There were bitter jokes.

Tepepe said, "They will take him to Cuernavaca where the lords of the law sit on their jack asses. They couldn't convict him here."

Tepepe found Timoteo. "Has your mama enough for a few days? Come with me. We are going to Cuautla. They must not be allowed to pull any tricks. Take him across and shoot him escaping. We must go with him across Wolf Canyon."

They traveled through absolutely empty fields, not a man in sight. Tepepe got very excited. It even gave him a thrill. He said to Timoteo riding behind him, "You see, without us they are nothing. You can see. Who is going to cut the cane and work in the mill? They know but we do not know that, without us, they are nothing. Now you see. Not a machete lifted, not an irrigation ditch opened for water. Nada, nada."

Timoteo said nothing, held on for dear life to the thin ribs of Tepepe, who was more like a strong rope than a man, hardly skin enough to tie the sheath of his vitals together, but leathered by time and sun, he could outride many a young man.

A terrible sight met them as they came into Cuautla. They saw Zapata in the midst of a squadron of armed horsemen of the military. He sat among them like some gay bird in his huge embroidered hat and his red embroidered charros. Timoteo and Tepepe joined the throngs that lined their passage, the soldiers' guns pointed at the ready, straight into their faces. There was hardly a sound. Sometimes Zapata seemed to lift his hand at some friend, or maybe it was just a fly. He rode erect, moving a little, very graceful with the movement of his horse.

Then Timoteo saw again the organization of the people for about two blocks behind the military convoy. Dressed as for a fiesta came his brother Eufemio, Montana, the Ink Pot, and about twenty others with all the silver on their horses, and the sun striking them, and the people's pleasure at seeing that they were going to accompany Zapata to Cuernavaca. Everyone began laughing, relaxed, and cheered them, but they felt they had best be quiet, not call too much attention. It tickled them to think of when the military would begin to get the nervous feeling they were followed.

Tepepe must have known of this all the time. He drew out his horse, and they fell into line behind Montana, and silently Zapata and the military, followed by the others, went between the rows of people that extended even out of town.

Along the road, they were never out of sight of people on horses, or standing at attention, in their hands the curved machete or an old gun, as if they had just come in from hunting. Sometimes a man and an oxen in his own field also would stop work and he would stand there with a gun.

Timoteo understood why the army had speeded up, and they were all going faster, at a trot, and he hung on to Tepepe. They went faster as all the villagers lined the roads as they went past, with sticks or rods or quirts. They said nothing, made no sound, just stood there. Timoteo got nervous at first when he could not see the cartwheel hat of Zapata, but then after a while he began to trust the people, to know that they would be standing up ahead. But what would happen when they came to the road of Wolf Canyon with its hairpin curves going higher and higher? A man could be murdered as his father was in an instant. He looked up and saw the buzzards following them. Even the buzzards knew the tricks of the army of Díaz.

At one place the priest had come out and stood in the church door. The women and children cried out jibes at the array, asking them if they had no father or mother or cursing them, or the little boys, getting bold, would cast a stone at the horses' hooves. But mostly they just stood there threatening. Once someone called Timoteo, and he recognized a boy who used to live in their village and had moved away. So this was where he had come. He solemnly raised his arm exactly like Zapata, and the boy raised his and they passed solemnly.

About noon they began to come into Yautepec. All the walls were covered with people. The streets were packed. People had come down from the north villages. Tepepe said, "There's a telephone here. This is the last place where they could call Cuautla or Cuernavaca for reinforcements. But wait and see," he said, smiling.

The army had stopped in the plaza, and the commander had gone to where the only phone in the town was. Eufesio and his little army had stopped on the opposite side of the plaza, and Montana was beckoning Timoteo, who slid off the horse's rump and ran over to the little hunchback, who looked fine and normal on a horse. He leaned down and gave Timoteo a package of cigarettes and a message for Zapata. Timoteo ran with the cigarettes into the pines where the boys were cutting up, trying to scare the horses of the army, and he began to shout what they were shouting and ran quickly between the horses and reached Zapata just as the commander angrily came out of the cantina, striking his lot with his riding whip, and he said to the next in command, "They have cut the telephone wires so there is no way of getting reinforcements from Cuernavaca. They will attack us in Wolf Canyon is my opinion."

Timoteo had given Zapata the message when he gave him the package that they would not attempt an attack on the canyon, that already plans were afoot to free him from the prison, if not legally, then some other way. A soldier had dismounted and grabbed Timoteo, and Zapata said, "Leave the boy alone. He only gave us a package of cigarettes from our friends. See for yourself." And he held out the package and the soldier started to take them, but the commandant said in a low voice, "Let him have them. Don't do anything to arouse these people." "Arouse," the other officer said, "a keg of dynamite with the fuse lit already. I don't like it." Timoteo was wedged in between the horses, and they had forgotten about him. "Our orders were to get him in Wolf Canyon, shot while trying to escape. If they don't get there before us and snatch him out of our hands. This would not be a good thing for us with the country as it is now."

Then Zapata, lighting a cigarette, said, "Why don't you kill me here, then my friends can at least bury me?" And the smoke came through his curved nostrils in a dangerous way.

"We'll bury you properly, never fear," one of the officers said, and the other one said, "The zopilotes are good enough for you."

"Fair enough," Zapata said, "They are the friends of all the corpses."

The commandant started walking over to Eufemio, and the crowd followed threateningly, and you could see that most of them carried their old guns. Timoteo darted back with the other little boys so nobody would spot him, and he heard the commandant say, "I order you to disband immediately and return to your villages."

"We are only a guard of honor," Eufemio said in his braggart way, "for my brother, as he has the honor of being so royally accompanied by you to join the army, to serve his father and which gives him the vote so freely."

Some laughed and some came closer with their guns. The commandant felt the hatred. "I order you to disband immediately."

Montana drove his horse up close to the commandant and looked on him. "You have no jurisdiction over us, Señor. I go there with my client to act as lawyer and interpreter."

"Well, what happens will not be my fault. He may be shot attempting to escape. You will be responsible if you attempt anything. Understand?"

"Perfectly," Montana said.

So the army gathered like a dun hive around Zapata, and they road past the old viaducts, and the people followed them out of town. Montana dropped back and asked Tepepe, did he think it was wrong not to try for it in the canyon. Tepepe pondered and said it was hard to say, and Timoteo wanted to cry, "They will kill him in the Wolf Canyon. It will be night before we get through. They will kill him like my father." He must have cried it out loud, for Montana put his hand on his knee. "We must have some legal moves. We will follow, you will see. He will be safe. Young Salino wants him for the races, and he has promised to come tomorrow and see if he can pay to have him released from the army services. He is after all Díaz's relative and will try to persuade him that the elections are over now, all is quiet, and Zapata is going back to the horses, and the sugar cane crop needs attention, and the mill will run again, and Morelos will be the sugar bowl of the world again, quietly sending out millions to people it never sees."

And Tepepe said, "We have our leaders here. We need every man here. You must have more faith in the people, Timoteo. The people will know how to protect their own."

And it was then that Timoteo did learn forever what the power and the skill of the people was.

Wolf Canyon was a low part of the mountains through which a river had gashed a deep erosion, and in spring it was full of water. It furnished water for the irrigation of the cane in the valley. It was good for grazing now after the rains, but the rest of the year was a semi-arid dry canyon of sharp hills through which a road had been built with hair-pin curves so sharp that accidents were common. There were some starving families that had carved out poor cornfields along the hills, but mostly at this time of the year only shepherds brought their flocks. They began to enter the canyon while the sun was still up, abruptly climbing on the narrow road where the horses had to go two by two. After you crossed the top, the road then descended into the wide valley in which the capital of Morelos, an old summer home of emperors and presidents, lay.

The sunlight fell behind them on the valley, and their last signs of Popocatépetl, and then they entered the canyon where the sun struck the near side at the top with light. And it was already night on the dark side, and the road would enter darkness more and more. Timoteo hated to leave the sight of the rosy snow-capped volcano that seemed at its base to float in blue scarves and rose now to its snow and rosy light over which Cortez had come to conquer them.

Then Timoteo had his lesson as they turned away from the valley and entered the first curve that turned so sharply, they lost sight of the big hat of Zapata for a moment and anxiously spurred up to pass the curve themselves. And there in their white calzones, strangely alight with their guns pointed, stood a row of men just above the canyon along the hills' lip, and they turned slowly, covering the caravan as they passed. When Timoteo passed them at the rear of Zapata's men, they uncocked their guns and moved off. Later he decided they were relays of men who mounted horses and appeared further on—all in their white loose pajamas and their bird-like hats, they began to glow in the darkness like some great birds come to save them. Around the small curve men sat on their little ponies and pointed their guns the same way. They could have killed every man in the caravan.

Timoteo almost shouted, "Look, look, around every hill!"

"Quiet, boy," Tepepe said, as if talking to a bad colt.

They rode on, and the light ceased on the eastern hill. The darkness seemed to rise like water from the canyon itself. The army was trying to go as fast as they could, but around every hill appeared this gleaming white flock of men with guns pointed and turning slowly to follow the men until they turned the next curve. The army began to know that these mysterious men would light before they turned the next curve and would be standing there, silent. Many of the soldiers were also farmers' sons, and they began to look sheepish, drooping in their saddles as if they would like to disappear. Timoteo thought their guns wavered and some seemed to let them by their side. Timoteo said, "See the men. It's getting them. We could take him now, just like nothing, just like taking an apple from a dead pig's mouth."

Timoteo could think of nothing he would wish for more than to see Zapata ride out of that mass of men that held him, chained and surrounded. He could see him gallop away, his horse nickering and dancing, and him raising his hat as he did when he was praised by the people for his feats of horsemanship. But they went on, and these white-dressed farmers glowed in the darkness that deepened in the canyons, and then the wonderful little fires began. They would turn the sharp curve, and there along the mountainside like some magnificent picture, the men would be standing with the little fires as their guns and white legs and the nickering muzzles of their horses, and sometimes picking out a face of boy or man, as if the fire also flamed in the faces from the heart.

Timoteo thought with pride, "These are my people, sons of Cuauhtémoc."

Chapter 11

Alfredo and Timoteo didn't see each other for a long time after the burial of Anaya. Alfredo went south with the guerrillas, and Timoteo went with a group of men, including Montana, who stayed around Cuernavaca while Zapata was imprisoned there. More and more, he had more serious missions, messages taken long distances. He even went to Mexico City afoot once to get the paper that came from the north, to see what was happening.

More and more, he took part in the political discussions held around the campfires at night. He formed opinions and was bold enough to express them, and the men listened to him. More and more, young men of his own age joined them, were taught the use of the machete by the older guerrillas. Also in the evening, those who knew a few letters taught the alphabet to those who knew nothing. There was a great desire to read. It had only just occurred to most of them that reading was not just a possession of their conquerors, but that they also might learn to read and know more than was going on before your noses, as they said.

They camped around the capital city, Cuernavaca, and there began to be a nervous feeling about Zapata since he did not come out, wasn't tried, and Salentino merely shrugged and seemed not to care if he got out in time to take his blooded horses to the races. The men were getting very nervous.

There was talk of how to get into the prison, how to see Zapata himself, to get a message to him. They sat around the fire tossing up ideas. The prison at Cuernavaca was an old dungeon built when Maximilian lived in Cuernavaca as his summer home and was guarded against assassins. When he came, all dangerous people—beggars, thieves—were caught up in a net and put away in the dungeons. So driving in his golden carriage with Carlotta, he would not be shocked to see them or endangered by any shouts or threats.

One night they decided that they must immediately get in and confer with Zapata, find out if he was alright, and tell him their plans and learn his.

"Timoteo," Montana said, "he must go. A boy can get into the prison where a man could not. They are all a mangy lot at the governor's palace, ready for any bribe. You can pretend to be begging, with this black pig bank for the church. Do you dare, boy, try to get to Zapata?"

"Yes," said Timoteo, shivering. "Yes, I dare." But as he was thinking that he had never been to Cuernavaca in his life. From where they had stopped just outside on the hill, he saw the city like a sparkling brooch on the valley's darkness, flickering like a thousand jewels, and smoke arose and he felt afraid. "How will I find the palace? I do not know the city. I have never been there."

The men all began to give him advice. "Just follow the streets. That city was the summer home of Maximilian and Carlotta, of Montezuma, of all the rulers. I guess Maximilian used to come from the capital driven by eight white mules. The palace was built for his wife, Carlotta."

"They didn't just build a little summer home. They didn't build it. We built it, yes, slaves built it. So you follow the birds to Carlotta's summer home. Remember that we shot her husband, Maximilian, who thought he could set up a French empire on our land. And the next time you go, remember it will be to see Governor Zapata and not that poor dusty campesino now growing in the darkness. You keep that in mind, boy, and walk and talk proud and bold, you hear?"

"Yes," Timoteo said, shivering in the dark, listening to all their advice. "Just follow the trail down a centuries-old trail of man and beast going to market. Take the first road turning left and follow the lights to the center. There you cross the devil's barranca, and you will see above it the biggest palace you ever saw. Underneath and behind it will be the jail."

"How will I know?"

"How does one know a jail? By the smell. By the darkness. By the curse men have put upon it unjustly imprisoned there. And the bars. If you can't sneak through the guards, then you will have to go back behind the stinking barranca, through an underground tunnel into the bottom of the stinking jail, crawl under the bars and through the bull pen. Give him the tequila if none of the thirsty guards get it from you, and tell him to act like a lamb, to put on a show, to let it be known that the election is over, that he has lost interest in politics, and that he is going to go with the horses of Salerno."

"Put on the lamb's wool," one of the men said, "over the lion."

"Tell him that. You remember?" Montana said.

"Yes," Timoteo said, shaking.

"Give the boy a serape. The kid is shaking," someone said. A dozen were held out, and Montana wrapped him in one and gave him the embrazo as between men, and he said "adios" very loudly. As if suddenly, he dropped out of the fire glow in immediate darkness with only the city sparkling in the cool night air and the path deep as Montana had said, marked well, and falling down towards the valley in the darkness, marked by centuries of men and animals coming across the Ajusco Mountains, bringing their goods, their pottery, their weaving, or coming like himself to get men out of jail or take messages of comfort or a little of the good tequila from the maguey plant to see a man through even torture.

In the darkness, the wind blew from behind him as if pushing him. A mountain wind does not blow continuously, but you hear it for a long time coming from behind you like an army running. Then it engulfs you, nearly knocks you down, then thunders on, leaving you in a hurricane of quiet. Then you hear it coming again, approach and engulf you and pass on again.

He held the serape over his mouth to keep from swallowing the bad airs his mother had taught him held demons and illnesses. She believed the evil one came out in the night and would enter the body and cause terrible and mysterious sicknesses. When he or his father used to come in at night from the pastures, she would pass an egg over their heads, rubbing it over their whole bodies down to the feet, taking out all evil airs, and then she would break the egg in a glass and throw it out into the dark, saying she had thrown away the evils.

He could not think of his mother. It made him seem unreal trotting through this strange darkness to a place he had never seen on a dangerous journey to take a message to a great man he loved. He seemed like someone he didn't know. To think of his mother made him think that he heard in the wind the mother of the poor dead child known all over Mexico who went crying in the wind at night, crying "ooooooo mi baby"—appearing wherever men were hanged, or where bandits had killed them, or looking into the faces of shepherds who died after her terrible gaze. Yes, now that he had thought of her, he was sure she had cried in the wind that had just passed him, half turning him with its ferocity, and he hid his face. Do not look into my face. I am not your child. What pity. What horror. Yes, she was flying down to Cuernavaca to look for her baby, or maybe it meant there had been death after they thought he was safe in the city. He began to run to outrun her, for she might believe he was her lost one. Something yanked at his serape and peered under his hat. "Don't, don't," he cried. "I am Timoteo!" But she ran beside him, her cold breath on him. "I am going to Cuernavaca. Cuernavaca," she moaned. Everyone knew she flew from the sea to the city, even up and down the streets of Mexico, crying,

crying. She cannot kill Zapata. No, he will tell her to go look for her dead child. "Go look for your dead child!" he cried, as Zapata would. "I am not he!"

He ran on. Would he never come to the turning? He remembered all the stories he had heard of how she goes deeper than a well to find all the dead men. Her voice comes in the night where no man recognizes his brother. She wears a heavy rebozo of wind—yes, wind—and when you pull it back you see nothing but a skeleton. So he did not touch the wind but seemed to be running through it. The lights of the city appeared and disappeared as he ran up and over the hills and then down into the valleys. But they seemed to grow brighter and larger, and he felt the wind moaning, being left behind as if it was afraid of light. He felt sorry and said to her, "Rest, Mamacita. I am going now into the lights and let you follow in the wind." He heard her moan as he left the dark hills now, saw them rise sharp against some lingering light, and knew the men were waiting around the fire. If he did not return, they would come after him. Now he had many fathers who protected him and asked him to do great deeds, which he could not refuse, even though he shook with fear.

As they had said, the road turned to the left sharply through some ruins, some haciendas where there were still gay lights, past some little stone houses built in a stone wall, and then the sharp turn into the paved street, a well-lighted road, and carriages drawn by great shining teams of the biggest horses he had ever seen, which made their hill ponies look like rabbits. Fancy-dressed drivers sat above the gleaming ladies and gentlemen in the carriages, and the silver on the harness gleamed and shook. He had entered a fairy land. He had to walk slow and look at everything. Every house was as big as the hacienda in Anenecuilco, all behind walls with gleaming light and sounds of music and voices and great blooming vines and trees perfuming the air, and no corn fields or sugar cane at all.

As they said, the streets narrowed and curved swiftly like paths, and he recognized the way the poor lived crowded together wall to wall, with vendors in the doorways selling oranges and nuts, which reminded him he was hungry. He took out a tortilla and ate it. He took off his serape, not seeing anyone wearing one, and he felt very countrified. Some people said "buenas noches" to him, and he answered, surprised. The city was warm with closeness and people and SHE had not followed him out of the wind into the city. He did not know how long he had walked.

He looked across a deep barranca where he could hear water running swiftly far down, and there he saw huge arches risen on the hill and knew it was the governor's palace. He kept his eyes on it until he rose up a sharp hill. There he was in the brightest lights he had ever seen, amidst an uproar of prancing horses being sharply reined so that rich ladies and gentlemen could get into their carriages. There were sharp cries and laughter. Some affair had taken place, and they were all going home. He must hurry. He took out his black pig from his rope bag. He stood across from the palace under a great tree where the birds moved uneasily and asked him why he was there, and he told them, "I am looking for the greatest man of our time named Zapata. He is hidden there in that stone. Some day you will lean out of your nests and see him ride up, a more splendid night than this."

Nothing to do but plunge in and see how the water was. He darted across the street. There was a yell. He covered his head, dodged back as he would at the lunge of a bull, animals reared close to him, the coachman swore at him, and some ladies with veils and jewels leaned out to see him as he cowered back, half falling against the hub of the wheel. A palace guard grabbed him by the collar, shaking him so hard the pig rattled.

"What are you doing here," the guard shouted.

Timoteo held up his black pig bank. "Just a beggar for Cristo," he said, "in the name of God."

The guard apologized to the ladies. "A god shaker crying for alms, just a lépero, a rascal."

"Why," one of the ladies said, "he is only a boy." "Here, here!" she cried to her husband, "give the darling boy something, out at this time of night on his holy errand." Timoteo grabbed off his hat as he had seen beggars do, bent his middle, and mumbled to himself, "If she only knew what his errand was." The coins tinkled in the pig's slot, and he bowed low, "Gracias, gracias, Señora!" And he heard her say to her husband, "You see, they are not so bad. It's ridiculous to think there is any danger in these people."

"Gracias, gracias," he bowed low after them, "may the holy Señor bless you and may the devil take you home," he added as the carriage drove on, and the guard said, "What's all that you say? You little ladrón, you have manners."

"Please, Señor," Timoteo cringed and bowed and thought what bribe would he take, "let me go in and ask the gentlemen for alms. It will be good for their souls, make them sleep better." He gave the guard a monstrous wink.

The guard laughed. "Mind you don't be a nuisance, and give me a cut."

He wasted no time, darted into the great lighted door where there was a drone of voices and fine gentlemen dressed like black birds he had often seen at Anenecuilco when he had held the horses for a few centavos. He looked frantically for any stairway leading downwards. How would he ever find him among all this dead and ominous stone? He saw a dark stairway and was about to dart down it when someone called, "This way, son." And he found himself in a throng of huge men taller than any of his race and frightening blonde, with blue eyes and strange laughter very loud and above him. They all gave him something, asking him where he was from, how much he had, why he wasn't in bed at this hour, and he answered, bowing, bowing, "Gracias, gracias, Señores."

At last they had their tall hats and, when they were not looking, he started down the stairs and found himself in a labyrinth of darkness, and he kept darting through doors and any stairs that descended. He heard men talking and some loud peasant laughter and thought these might be the prison guards. Then he saw a small charcoal fire in a brazier and smelled the smell of roasting goat's meat and saw the guards with meat on the ends of their swords and a bottle of tequila, from which they drank. He tried to look as small and frightened as he could and cried, "Oh, Señores, I am lost. I am trying to collect a few centavos for our suffering Lord. The padre sent me."

"Look what we have here, a little collector from God. Let's put some tequila down his gullet and see how he dances."

A big kindly fellow said, "Oh, he's just a baby. You little bugger, so you want a few coins. Looks like a little carne would put some meat on your ribs. Why look, you can count his ribs."

"Señor," he said to the big fellow who handed him a piece of meat at the end of his sword, "let me collect from the prisoners for the good of their souls. The padre says it gives them a chance for redemption. To give a few centavos, they have may save their souls."

"Why, you innocent, do you think they leave them here with any centavos. After we get through going through them, they don't even have fleas."

"Maybe he's trying to get in to see that Zapata, that rascal."

"I never heard of him," Timoteo said.

"Won't serve his time for the good of his country. Why not let the little fellow go in and preach to them? Do them good if they have any souls. Go ahead open the door." A huge key turned the lock, and they pushed open the heavy door. "How do you know we won't keep you there? Just pound on the door when you're ready to come out, and if we're not asleep we'll let you out. And if we are asleep, well, you may never get out. The guard will change and you'll just be a prisoner like the rest. Too bad for you. You'll have to serve time for your good deeds which many a cristiano has done before you. You'll go to heaven for your suffering, me young buck." He was thrust through the door, and it clanged behind him. He could see nothing. He seemed to have been thrown into a bottomless pit. At first he thought it was a joke of the guards. Before he could see anything, a voice quite near startled him, saying, "Timoteo?" It was both a question and a salute.

It was the voice of Zapata.

Chapter 12

He could hardly make anyone out. It was a damp dungeon, very dark and cold. Many were sleeping in what seemed to be hay scattered on the floor. Zapata seemed to draw him into the dark with his gleaming eyes alive as a cat's. He whispered, "Zapata?" The iron door had shut behind him, and he could hear the drunken guards laughing and singing. Zapata came swiftly and took him by the shoulders and lifted his face up. "My chico, Timoteo," he said, caressing his head, and then abruptly, almost taking his breath away, embracing him and holding him close. "Come over here to the corner. The little thieves in here are asleep. Our friends are in another cell. Talk low, though, they have spies here. There are no alacrans like in Durango, though the scorpions here are friendly." They went over to an angle in the heavy stone walls that were sweating water dripping from them. Zapata looked at him hungrily. "What did you bring? Why did you come? How did you get in here, my brave one?"

Timoteo laughed and from under his serape took the package topped by his begging alms. "I was a beggar," he said. "The compadres are camped in Wolf Canyon. They are worried about you. Here," and he handed him the tortillas and the tequila. Zapata eagerly gulped down a long drink and then wolfed the tortilla. "Tequila is as good as twelve sheepskins," he said.

"I got in here," Timoteo said, "as a beggar in the name of God."

Zapata embraced him again. "Good, good, your mamacita will be proud—in the steps of your father."

"I ran with the moaning woman after me. I came past the great houses, the palace of Maximilian and Carlotta I had heard about."

"We all know fear. The brave man simply has more fear and makes more courage." He took another drink of tequila and whispered, "Did you hear of the country where there was such a dry season that the maguey were dying, and they watered it with their tears, and then with the blood of tigers and parrots and peacocks, then their own blood, and at last they killed the bulls and the hogs to keep alive the maguey. It made a delicious tequila, but when you drink it you become peacocks and parrots and you grow fierce and angry when you get to the tiger's blood. Finally, when you come to fix it, men become hogs, and they had to destroy the maguey that it came from. It cuts the cold, though. What time is it, lad?"

"The time of God?" Timoteo was feeling good now. "The official time which is the time of coyotes and hacks of government and prison keepers, or the astronomical time? It is about midnight, for all the fancy people, the tall-legged and the blancos are just going home from the palace."

Zapata laughed and now he was becoming clear in the dark, his sharp face and the huge black eyes and the black mustachios that hid his mouth. "I thought I heard the sound of horses through the stone. The stone tells you everything. If I was here long enough, I would make a study and would know where every stone came from. I would know the quarry. And, yes, even the home of the workmen whose brawn and mallet cut them and laid them so cunning, for a Frenchman who had the nerve to come here to take our land, our stone and our labor. You must know our history, Timoteo, to be so brave."

"It is not hard to be brave when you see our people like they were the day they brought you into Cuernavaca, standing there around each turn of hill, cutting the telephone wires."

They both began to laugh, and Zapata drew them down to the floor, made of dirt and cold. "Yes, out of the heart of each it comes. A man is made like these rocks from the ancient history, from the volcano heat, from the dust, from the work and sweat and salt. What else did you bring me?"

"Messages," Timoteo said, his face becoming severe as he tensed to remember everything. He pushed back the dust on the floor and began to quickly draw the map in his mind. Seventy men waited for him to get out of prison, between Cuernavaca and Cuautla. They had already intercepted one train and were well supplied with huertas, guns, ammunition, clothes and food. Zapata could hardly contain his delight. "You mean my little white rabbits, the humildes, waited for a train from Mexico loaded with the weapons meant to annihilate us, rub us out, and they took them all and turned them in the other direction?"

Timoteo nodded. "And here." He showed the taking of two towns in Guerrero, the army fled, and the people set up their own government at Chilpancingo. A delegation had come from Michoacán and pledged their support. Burgos had gone south into the state of Oaxaca to organize the rebellion there. News from the north was that Madera was setting up a government in Mexico City, and Huerto would be withdrawn from Morelos. He was known as the most murderous general, to whom a campesino was less than a louse. He left a trail of hanged wherever he went, and pits of the dead.

"If Madera has a program to give the land back to the people, then he is our man. We will have to find out."

"Well, it is said that he is for the people. His program is for all voting."

"The franchise, yes, and no one is to be elected twice. It is good, but it is not even a beginning."

"Yes."

"The Indian people have to be rescued from their hunger and their landlessness."

"Yes, Tepepe says the norteamericano, what was his name, Abe Lincoln, said for the people by the people of— What was the other?"

"I do not know," Zapata said. "It is enough of the people—"

"That's it!" Timoteo laughed. "Of the people by the people for the people."

Zapata repeated it. "A fine saying. Juárez said that too. He loved that Lincoln. It was said they looked alike even. Now, what is to be done, my little wise man?"

"You are to put on the lamb's face. Cease the roaring and assure the judge that the elections are over, and that you are going back to taking care of the haciendados' horses."

"The hell you say!"

"Montana says and tomorrow or the next day Salerno will come with money to beg for you to get off to take his horses to the races, to say you are the only one who can handle them."

"Aye," said Zapata, calming down, "this sounds well. As the ox driver says: little by little we go far." He began to sing in a low voice.

> Companions of the plow,
> Enslaved and starved and dirty.
> There is but one road now.
> Grab your thirty thirty.

"Pipe down!" a sleeper bellowed, and Timoteo whispered, "Remember the lamb."

"Aye, remember the lamb in us all and also remember the lion."

They were quiet, and then Timoteo said, "When will we make the plan?"

Zapata was startled. "The plan?"

"Yes," Timoteo moved closer to his ear, "you have to have a plan. That is, what are you going to do when you win? You have to have this plan so the people can take it out and look at it."

"Oh yes, I see," Zapata whispered back. There was another silence. "Timoteo, what do you want?"

"Well, the first and the middle of the last thing is land."

"That is the first. Some say it would be liberty, freedom. In the American revolution in the north, which I have tried to learn as much about as I can from the learned, the correctos, the readers, is that one of their leaders said very early, 'Give me liberty or give me death.' "

Timoteo thought and then he said, "What is liberty? How can I ask for it when I have never had it and don't know what it is?"

"Why, that is true, it is certainly true. None of us know what it is. So which comes first? It is no problem. It is the land. The land is everything."

"This is very clear. No such great talk of liberty. Could we say then, as something for man to truly follow—Tierra y Libertad?"

"Yes, you could say that. Every man would understand, because he would just hear land, and the liberty would just follow like the coyote's tail."

"Very clear. You have given me a lesson."

"It comes to me I have forgotten some things, but they follow. Like houses and learning and cleanliness and being together like families. It will all come when we have our land again. We haven't had liberty for three hundred years, so how could we know about it? And we live in blind night without news, without reading."

Timoteo was afraid to ask it. "Can't you read, Emiliano? I thought maybe you could read when you held up the paper."

"It was a trick. I went to school two years. I learned a little but soon forgot it. Can you read in your watermelon field, riding a horse across the country six nights and days? What you do learn fades away because you cannot use it. Can you read, Timoteo?"

"I did the same thing as you, Zapata. I held up the paper and I didn't lie. I didn't say I could read, but I really pretended. I made everyone jealous." They leaned their black heads together, laughing without making a noise, for you never knew when the government planted stool pigeons in the bull pen to ferret out what the prisoners were thinking.

"Maybe you heard about that American president Juárez was so crazy for who was born in a log house, they say, and had a hard time learning to read too. You can be President, Emiliano, without knowing how to read. Besides, how many readers can you have? You have many readers, and it is not necessary for you to read."

"No, you are wrong, Timoteo. All must learn how to read. The women, too."

"The women? Who, of course, the women?"

"Who should read the most? The women because then they can teach the young. Why, I see it clearly. Why couldn't we start schools right now? Why do we have to wait? The readers can begin teaching and every day, say, a muchacho like yourself could teach another what you learned that day. Pretty soon we would have an army that could read. Why not?"

"Shhhhh," Timoteo warned Zapata, who always moved and shouted when he got excited. "A good idea. We will do it. Then it will be understood better which comes first, liberty or the land."

"How does it seem to you, Timoteo?"

"Well, Tepepe and I, being shepherds, we have had much time to think about it, and it seems to us that first in the plan is the land. Because when you have the land, everything follows that. Then you have food. No use liberty without food. How can it be? Then you have schools maybe and other things I do not even know about, and you don't even name liberty because it follows. Like the coyotes' game when they sing. 'Let's go to the blue corn to make stole,' and they sing, 'The tail—the tail! It is not of bone.' "

"Yes, it is important that I get out of here. There are going to be rumors. I must appear and squash them. This afternoon the governor offered me a hacienda if I would deliver all our arms over the Huerta and tell the campesinos to go back to work in the sugar and be nice quiet rabbits."

"They offered you a hacienda?"

"Yes, the great estate at Yautepec, Hacienda Atlihuayan. One of the greatest. They do not think we are of no account or of little account."

"What did you say, Emiliano?"

"I said I did not enter the revolution to make myself a haciendado. I want that land returned to my people, every milpas returned. Now, you rascals, before my people have received one parcel of land, you want to bribe and destroy us. If you gave me the whole of Morelos, there would still be a revolt. It is not myself, Emiliano Zapata, who has made this revolution. I am not the general. The general is named General Hunger. Hambre. Hunger. It is the people who have made the revolution, and they will win it. Now they will spread it around that they offered me the great hacienda, and it will be suggested that I have taken it. It will spread like wildfire, with their spies and wolves among the sheep. So say I will do as they ask. I will wrap my roars in the lamb's skin."

They embraced again. "I must be getting out. I will shake the bars and you pretend to be very angry that I asked for alms for God."

"Wait," said Zapata, "see that crack up there? For some reason there must be a balcony there on a courtyard. At any rate, the morning light makes a white crack there. If they do not remember you before, it would be better if there was a little light. They would not kill you so easily. Rest, mi chico hijo, rest, my brave heart."

Zapata drew his head to his shoulder, and Timoteo said the prayer his mother had taught him.

But the crack of light had not appeared before the drunken guards with great banging opened the doors and yelled, "Where's the little ladrón, the léperos, little thief of God? Vamanos!"

"Get him out of here!" Zapata yelled. "To ask alms of us poor and forgotten!"

They snatched Timoteo by the neck and lifted him out, the doors clanging.

Chapter 13

Timoteo licked his bowl of caba (goat) stew and felt warm and full, and the fright of his return over the mountains to the camp of the guerrillas seemed like a victory in him. He kept hearing the hoofs sound of horses coming from the east, west, north, south, as the guerrillas kept coming in to report how the villages were being taken over from the haciendados one by one, as far west as Guadalajara. Alfredo was set to hobbling their horses as they brought them in, taken from the haciendados, and cries went up as men recognized their horses of the patrons, embraced them, slapping them on the rumps, crying out, laughing, "Now, my beauties, you are of some use, not for showing off at fiestas, or for the fat rumps of men who do nothing. You are now in the army of freedom." And some hung evergreen boughs on their necks. Timoteo went to help stack the guns they also brought, taken from caravans, trains, and forts. Alfredo was excited and cried out to Timoteo, "Now you see all these treasures have been used only for luxury, for men and women who live in palaces. Now they belong again to the people who toil, those who produce the sugar cane and the fine horses."

He and Alfredo made marks down on the records of how many guns were stacked, and they were still not enough for the men who were gathering in the mountains. The little Ink Pot had said earlier that there were now three thousand men and three hundred guns.

"It is now five hundred," Timoteo said, bringing the paper to the Ink Pot, who sat around the council fire with the Mansanao brothers.

Another band came in whooping and hollering, and they had bundles of tortillas still warm sent by the women of the villages.

The talk flew swiftly from group to group as they stood lighted only by the fire and their faces glowed. Many came to Timoteo to ask about Zapata, how did he look, what did he say, and they embraced him warmly and looked at him with warm eyes. The lookouts cried out "Vaya con Dios" as they gave the password and were let into camp. Scouts were coming and reported to the leaders, who sat around Montana and Tepepe and the little Ink Pot, who had to read whatever they brought to him—clippings from papers, messages.

Timoteo was waiting to make a full report to the meeting which would be held later, when the full moon rose over Popcatépetl, whose white head they could see now to the east.

He must have dozed off with the food and the heat and his safe return, for when he woke he found he was sitting in the valley of a circling hill of men. The fire had been stacked with mesquite and even dried cacti and flickered on the faces that circled him—like a human hill all in their white calzones. He saw faces he knew, and faces that were like the ones he knew. He couldn't believe that these were the bent over, burdened and silent people he had known all his life. It wasn't the fire from outside that lit them as much as the fire that burned in them all, the fire that had accumulated in those years of abuse and violence.

It seemed a dream they were ever called the humildes. They looked as if they rose devouring the air like the fire did. The Ink Pot sat with a stump in front of him and around him the Jefes, many who had risen with the past week from the ranks of their villages or region. Solemnly they listened as one after another rose to make his report: how the people were cacheing arms in the mountains, and some had taken to the hills awaiting the plans of Zapata. Every kiln in the forest was an armed outpost. The delegates from Michoacán far to the west were waiting for Zapata and, besides, were ready to storm the prison and free him. Runners from Guerrero reported they had already taken the main town in that state, easy as snaring rabbits.

The dinameteros reported. Some rose and came in to hear them. They would have to train some of the young men. Most of them were old miners who knew how to work with dynamite, and they would teach one person from every place, and they in turn could teach others. They were tough old men with smashed and broken faces where the stones had fallen on them. But they knew their business. Thickset southerners, squat, burst, bloody, and powerful.

The old guerrillas from the battle of Puebla told the secret of guerrilla warfare. The Yankee guerrillas did that, fought a well-armed and well-fed army from the hills, never allowing them to shoot direct, coming out of the hills on the Red Coats, armed themselves from their enemies. Like us they were poor, had few guns, barefoot too many of them, and poorly clothed. The winters up there were worse than here. We will do that, outwit him, jump out at him, bush flank him, draw him, tease him, cut back on him, march on his rear, lure Huerta south then vanish. He will be in the jaws of an enemy he can't see. So what no one would think for you to do, never let up, whip them and whip them until they leave us alone. Let the drunk Huerta beat the empty air, attack him when he is drunk. Make the army sleepless, worm them out. They were told to wipe out the valley, destroy every village. Well, we will rise up in their teeth. Never engage them openly, draw them into traps that close on nothing, nothing.

Some men will travel alone. Rely on your own judgement or small groups or planned forays. Larger groups, like the seizing of the trains tonight, spring out of the old mills, fade away and plant corn.

One old man said he was asked if he was a Zapatista. "Why," he said, "even the stones cry Zapata. The whole countryside is an enemy to Huerta. The stones fall on him."

While you live, you raid the enemy, not the people. They will feed you. Sleep or raid, get supplies, capture enemy mule packs, plow, hoe and gun.

Huerta, driven north back to Mexico City, left them guns and ammunition. The people had already set up a provisional government and were drawing up the plan of the revolution and wanted to have it ratified and joined by the other states, both north and south.

They all looked at these delegates with awe, and some came down to embrace them, and Vivas were squelched with loud hisses for quiet lest they be discovered by some wandering Rurales.

A delegation had been north trying to get in touch with Madera who they said had a plan for the revolution and to unite the country, but they had not found him.

There were more reports, and it was an amazing picture Timoteo could not comprehend. How had they all caught fire at the same time? Not even from each other, as if some secret fire had been waiting only to be set. A phantom army had become a reality. He looked around at the many fathers who seemed to be leaning down to him, smiling, as he stood up on his tired legs to make his report, telling how he got through. There was laughter and men slapping their legs in pleasure at his cunning, and he had never felt so fine in his life.

When he told the reports that Zapata had been offered one of the finest haciendas to betray the people, to tell them to go back to the sugar mill and their milpas, his answer to them brought a sigh like a big wind in the trees as each man's body relaxed in pleasure at the purity of their leader. He said, "Suppose I took your watch. I would make you pay rent for the time you used it. But," Zapata said, "the land was not a luxury like a watch, it was land, it was life itself, that meant homes, beans, tortillas, corn. We want that land back. We want it now." It was agreed that the rumour of his taking the hacienda at Yautepec had already spread among the people. Many said this was so, nodding their heads in the firelight, and how important it was for Zapata to be freed quickly and appear among the people.

When the moon was high above popo [Popocatépol], Montana rose to make a little lecture, as he always did, and they listened respectfully. "Our duty," he said, "is to the people themselves, to the people of the villages, the peons, the campesinos, all the poor, who are our main support. We must behave like brothers. Do not destroy the haciendas either, for we want to return them to the people. There will be no looting or drunkenness, no molesting the women. The villages will share with us their arms and food. In the haciendas, take all the food, arms and horses you can find. We will need much food now we are gathering an army. Such an army as ours is an army of the people. We cannot live except as the people, like a mother nourishes us. And we must obey our leaders now. It is no longer every man for himself, except what you must endure alone. You must look out for yourself, you must obey. You, the man who disobeys, is a traitor to his comrades. Each man must endure until we win. And you must obey the jefes. You can vote them out and replace them. Any man who does not obey is a traitor."

Then Tepepe said, "Good talk. Now what we are going to do?"

"Tip the sugar bowl," someone shouted. "Muy bien!" others shouted. "The train goes through at dawn, within a mile of here. Dump the sugar into the barranca. Should we do that, all that sugar we helped grow? It is no longer ours. They will have plenty of guns and ammunition too. We have to have more guns, and dynamite, the dinamiteros said."

"Do not shout," Montana said. "Talk low. This is the way the North American revolution started, with just the farmers with their rabbit guns, I've heard, wouldn't pay a tax. Dumping some—tea, was it?—tea that belonged to the British hacienda, dumping it into the harbor. Did they do that? We will dump sugar. No more sugar. All the world gets sugar from Morelos, and when they hear that the workers dumped it, threw it into the barranca so they will have to pay more, yes, they will ask what was the matter. They will be interested."

Someone came forward and made a map of the barranca where the sugar train would come around the curve. The men were assigned places, fell into groups, mostly the men from Morelos who knew the ground like the palm of their hand. Timoteo was to be with four men from Cuautla he did not know well, only their faces on market day.

Timoteo looked around at them in the pre-dawn light. He saw the men he had seen all his life. He was shaking inside and stood close to them for their strength. They were not thieves or invaders. They were men who knew every path and corn milpas and had in their flesh the mark of every ledge, mountain, hidden valley, that could hide and screen a man, and where warmth and water were to survive. Some of them, forty in all, were hidden along the barranca, their guns pointed down the track. Sometimes he saw their ancient faces within the leaves of the bushes, bearing the mark of ancient Toltec. He and four men from Cuautla left the others and went towards where, if the train stopped, they would hold the engineer and fireman under their fire while the men behind dumped the sugar and took guns and ammunition.

From then on, he did not think or know fear. He was swept in an operation with others and he was amongst them, they surrounded him. He started loping with five others. One was a young boy like himself he did not know or had not seen. They went swiftly across the road, going steadily south, until they squatted above the railroad track where the engine would appear around the bend, coming slow up a grade. They knew exactly how fast it would be going and how quickly it would stop before the rest of the train had even begun to come around the bend. They heard the train coming slowly, slower than they had thought, which meant there were three or four more cars than they expected, which meant more food and guns.

Timoteo just looked at the curve with all his being, his gun gripped in his hands. They were to run down, shoot the two guards on top of the cab. If they were in luck, the engineer would be expecting them and stop the train. Perhaps that was why he was coming so slow. If another engineer had not been put on...be careful and do not shoot a compadre. It was a man he was not sure he knew.

The cow catcher thrust its snoot around the curve like some strange beast, and they slid down the hill onto the tracks. The two guards were clearly outlined against the sky, which was lighting with dawn. They fell soundlessly and the train stopped. They were in luck. The engineer called out the name of his friend and jumped out of the cab. He also had a gun. They were to simply see that no one came around the corner.

They heard the shooting as the train was held up. Then the shooting stopped. They must be loading the buns and food on the mule packs now. They would leave the train. They had heard The Villa took over all the trains in Chihuahua. He had such great plains to cross with his men. But they did not want the train. Only their life depended upon the food and the guns and ammunition and, also, to keep them from getting to the fort in Cuernevaca to be used against them. It would give them great pleasure to shoot the bullets meant for bodies into their enemies.

The signal was a coyote yell, and they were to return to the camp, the government. They squatted there and told the engineer what had been happening, and he told them about Cuautla, how the soldiers were afraid to appear on the streets and never came out at night, even for a girl or a drink.

Then they heard the coyote yelp, and they tore up the side of the hill, the engineer with them, who would never drive an engine again, and got back to the camp, which had even more people in it. The mule packs were returning, and Zapata had come back. He was talking to the delegates from Michoacan. They sat like a strange circle of men under the May trees, serious, their gestures and silences full of portent.

He saw Alfredo, who looked as if he had been dipped in soot, blackened from the engine, and he began to laugh, and he and Alfredo gave each other such a fierce abrazo they could have broken a rib.

"Zapata's back! He is among us again!" And now they seemed to be crying, but hid their faces in each other's shoulders.

Chapter 14

Timoteo was waiting for Zapata to go with him to the Jujutal, where the people would be gathered to see if Zapata was out of prison.

Zapata was known and loved for his paso de la muerte, a symbol of their avowal of the clean wild hardihood and skill, daring and fearless of death with which they had survived four hundred years of terrible servitude. They loved Zapata for his timing and the freedom and pride of love they saw in his brilliant figure as he would leap from a running horse to the horns of a running bull and throw him, or grab him by the tail and throw him. Timoteo held his horse in the wooden passage on the other side of which they could hear the thumping of the wild bull. Zapata's horse could hardly be curbed waiting for the wooden gate to open at the same time as the bull's gate was opened, and the horse with Zapata would have to time the run exactly with the bulls, or the horns would pierce the rider to death.

Timoteo was to meet Zapata on the Sierra by the river of Ayala and was squatting in the brush, watching the road as it turned down the high sierras, so he could spot Zapata and see who would be with him and if anyone was following. He could see the horse path as it wound down, and the horseman would come into view and then pass out of view as he descended to the road. He was drawing letters with a stick and spelling out the Plan of Ayala–Tierra y Libertad–which he could spell now.

There were many things to think about. He felt for Tepepe's horn, which he was now to play for the Diana at the paso de la muerte in place of Tepepe.

That very morning they had seen Tepepe disappear on a black horse from the hacienda, taking the mountain road north, to get in touch with Madera and find out what his land program was and if they should support him. They were not a band of rascals seizing sugar cane and land, but an organized army disciplined with ammunition. Taking back their own, Tepepe had said he was not the one to go, not being able to read. "No, Tepepe is the one," Zapata had said. "He can get through the mountains, take the train north to Saltillo as a vender. We need a man who has good legs and guts and knew every tree and cave and can pass for shepherd or ladrón and get through the cities. You we trust and the land trusts you, the chica tierra, our little brother, the land men like you alone know her truly.

Tepepe straightened as if new youth flowed into him, and he turned and embraced Zapata. "I am that one, then, but who will blow the bugle while I am gone?"

"I am that one," Timoteo said.

"You are the one, then, to blow the Dianna." Zapata had put an arm around him. "My generals will all be over sixty and under sixteen," he laughed.

Montana taught Tepepe the message by heart so nobody could get it out of him or find it on him, never to repeat it to anyone but Madera, who would be waiting in the north.

"Waiting for me?" Tepepe laughed.

"Yes, and he will learn you a message to bring back to us, his program, his plans, his ammunition."

His mamacita washed his calzones to a fine whiteness, and with his rope bag and sarape, he set out over Popocatépetl, through the valley to the train on the other side. They all embraced him, knowing the dangers of the trip. If he did not come back, they would know the tortures he had been put to.

Timoteo unwrapped his bugle and rubbed the shine in, spit on his thumb and rubbed it lovingly.

Then he saw Emiliano Zapata weave in and out the mountain path, and he had a fine spotted pony he was leading. Had he found the pony, or killed the man who rode it? Timoteo watched him come, sitting on his fine horse better than a king, he thought, and he rose smiling to take the bridle. Zapata looked down, his black eyes flashing, pushing back his embroidered sombrero, and Timoteo saw he was dressed for the paso in his tight embroidered pants and his boots, as if poured into them, and his bright braided jacket and, above all, his face flashed like a sword above him.

"Timoteo, scout and citizen, your mount."

Timoteo didn't know what a mount was, but he knew a horse when he saw it.

"Did you borrow it?" he said slyly, with that accent on "borrowed."

"Don't stand talking like a school teacher. Get on. We've got a ride to Jojulta."

"Mine!" Timoteo said, mounting, and Zapata already galloping into the mountain trail, he followed, for the first time riding a running horse who had had much money on his head at the races. As they rode along, he felt for the first time alone on a horse that had a good run and a gallop. He rode just behind Zapata, holding onto his hat, which he finally removed and hung on the saddle horn. He was breathless and felt like hollering and laughing as he kept up with Zapata, and he tried to copy his seat and hold the horn under his blouse with one hand. He would never tie it to the horn for fear it would get a dent in it. The dents were all Tepepe's and would become his own only in battle.

Outside Jojutla, the roads were crowded with the people who turned to cheer Zapata as he passed, cheers for the horseman who would risk his life that day, or for the man who would, before he was assassinated, lead them for nine years into a new nation.

Timoteo caught up and rode alongside his jefe and couldn't help but bow a little at the cheers and greetings.

"We've got to show the people that I am out of prison, that the rumors about my being bought off are false, and the election is the last one they will steal. The Jaripeo, the paso de la muerte, will be the first grita that we are a people in arms. The whole country will be in arms in twenty-four hours. We will not only have generals, Timoteo, like yourself and Tepepe, but an army fighting for freedom."

"I pray to God it will be so," Timoteo said, bowing, and it seemed to him his horse also bowed. "Díaz will be alarmed that we are winning."

"Listen carefully, my little amigo, now. Zapata's face was drawn to a sharp look, and he smiled at Timoteo. "If my horse does not come after the bull is down, you ride in and bring him, then the Diana to get the people's attention. I will speak from the back of the horse, and then you must be ready to open the back gate. We must join the others in the hills. If I get lost, it is by the big organ cactus. You know the one."

They looked at each other. It all happened, as always, so fast, like everything good, beautiful, and fast. You had to do it in one moment or not at all. It was like blowing the bugle too. You put everything into that moment, entirely. Tepepe said it was just a piece of time and a piece of an inch between blowing the bugle, putting your lips to the mouthpiece, and not blowing the bugle at all, making no sound. You had to catch the bull by the horn, stop him, thrust your fingers into his nostrils, get a leverage before he knew you were after him at all, before he gathered his strength against you. Many, many men had been killed thus, and suddenly Timoteo thought, how stupid to risk the life of a man like Zapata. But it would get the people's attention. Would they ever forget the stretched-out horse, the fine rider in his fine clothes in the afternoon sun, risking his life as he would to the end of it?

The quiet became frightening. He almost forgot his role in the drama. He put the hot horn to his mouth, and the noise startled him, and his new little horse shook, her pelt rippling like water, but she stood. When the last note sounded, he heard Zapata saying something like, "Hah!" to his horse, and they both leapt away from him into the light. There was the black bull thundering with them, shaking the earth as Zapata's horse leapt entirely into the run, laid out straight, timing herself to the bull's run as he gathered speed, feeling followed. Neck and neck they went. The crowd was tense, quiet, and the sun was just right, with no shadows and not in Zapata's eyes. Then it was so sweet, so fast he could not follow. He saw the horse galloping free without Zapata, and the dust torn up where the man and bull met, collided and held. He had got him, and he saw the man pull back, the bull skid to a stop, and both hold in a moment of equal strength against each other. He had made the pass so dangerous and now must with strength throw the massive body allied against him.

The dust settled in the light around them, and thousands of eyes seemed to rivet them there. Then slowly, at first you could hardly tell, but the massive wrinkled neck of the bull began to turn, pivot on its body, and the slender hips seemed badly made to hold him to earth, to pin him down. The man was like a lever with some strength coming from the ground, in which his feet seemed planted. The powerful, steady pressure began to turn the diminishing rear of the bull, the black rumps turned like a screw. At last, with one flood of energy, he fell helpless, lay back in the dust and sunlight, and the crowd broke loose in a mighty roar and started towards Zapata. He held the bull until others ran out with ropes to fasten him.

Timoteo had been so stunned he had not watched the horse, but now saw that he pranced up and returned to his master, who brushed his clothes, mounted and held up his hands, looking for the forgotten Diana that Timoteo was to blow. He got the thought and quickly drew in his breath, gathered himself, and went out into the horn. The people stopped, surprised. Zapata's horse reared on his hind legs, and Zapata drove him into the people and motioned them close around him. They obeyed him as horses did and poured around him, and he started out, breathing heavily yet, and as if speaking was harder than the paso de la muerte. He named them all. "Señores, Señoritas, Humildes, Compadres, Campesinos." As the unnamed were named, they stopped and turned their faces upward into the light of this man among them.

"I speak to you," he said, breathing hard, "from ages of silence." And they saw the facile, the magnifico, the romantic idol of rodeos and the guitar, fond of gay clothes and pretty girls, suddenly rise on his horse in an awful vision, erect, calling them out to perform a difficult and noble act. "Blind men in blind night," he told them who now stood in the light of history, slaves illiterate and dispossessed now had the power to back their own. They had a paper, *Regeneración*, and he told them what that word meant. To generate, to make grow, to regenerate, to make grow again. He named all the allies this paper gave them, the regions and the people and Madera coming down from the north to join them. He said, "We are going to arm now. The time has come."

Timoteo could see the people were amazed, as if they had jumped a hundred years ahead in time, as if suddenly, out of darkness, intelligence seemed to emerge from their faces. He could see what the words could do, like a potter upon his clay. Words were not just for church or Sunday. Words were powerful, like wind upon sleeping fire in the charcoal blowing up the memory of woods. Words, he saw, could be blown into actions, and actions were brutal without the words, which meant something you could not see or touch but were real in the heart of man. They meant that everyone could fight for the same thing. Freedom, he could see, was a word you didn't have to understand. It was a mighty force. Perhaps men had made it mighty fighting for it always in different ways. The words suddenly became hard, like fruits in season out of darkness, hanging, made visible upon the tree.

Then Zapata did not speak too long. He timed it exactly as you had to do in connection with the bull's horns: the fire was just ready to blast out of smoke and confusion, and their understanding stood open. He stood in his stirrups and coined the phrase for which they were to fight for nine long years. He shouted, "Tierra y Libertad! Land and Liberty!"

There was a startled silence for a moment as it fell like hot steel into the water of their minds. Then they seemed to flame up as they shouted, "Viva! Viva! Viva! Tierra y Libertad!" three times before there was screaming in the rear of the crowd, cries of women, "The Rurales! Run, run!" They had come into the village without their uniforms, and they now rode brutally toward Zapata, uncovering their guns, bayoneting the people out of their path. It was amazing how swiftly they were led through, the people flowing behind them, closing them off, opening before them until they rode at a gallop through the back gate. But there fifty horsemen were waiting for them and surrounded Zapata. Timoteo's little horse bolted, and thought him of no importance.

Zapata cried out, "Don't shoot. Stop your men in their bayoneting children!"

"You are under arrest," the commander said.

"Have you papers?"

"The army of Díaz does not need papers to arrest for sedition and rebellion. The mayor of Jojutla has been hanged under my orders."

"Under my orders. You have seen here that I have just entertained the people with the paso de la muerte. Since when has that become treason? I do not recognize your authority to arrest us. You are local police of Morelos. I will recognize no authority but those of Díaz himself.

Timoteo saw Montana riding off, and he sat on his horse like the spectators, the army held back, making a wall with their guns pointed.

"I want no massacre of women and children such as you brave ones showed us in Anenecuilco the day you helped steal the election. Take me bound to the Zócalo, and I will wait until you get the proper arrest papers from Díaz. All you have to do is phone the capital." He stood in his stirrups, speaking to the people. "We will all go to the Zócalo, where these gentlemen are going to phone the President. I will submit only to the Federales."

The people nodded approval and felt some cunning in it, and also the disguised Rurales were getting nervous. "Don't be nervous." Zapata knew some of them had known him all his life. "When we get to the Zócalo, you can tie me up." Some of the people stayed, afraid for him, and he spoke to them. "Am I your jefe? Then do as I say. Have confidence. Let them tie me up. Do nothing."

When they got to the Zócalo, a young man tied him to the water trough with a leather thong, and the women began to mourn and cry and make an awful noise, and some knelt praying and tried to kiss his feet. He brushed down his hair and smoothed his mustache. Timoteo had learned to wait until he was usable. Sure enough, Montana sitting on his horse did not turn to look at him but said in a low voice, "Eufemio and a hundred men are just outside on the other side of the organ cactus. Ride like the devil and bring them here." Timoteo turned his horse and let it walk out of the crowd, not to attract attention.

There was no guard leaning out, and he saw the one telephone wire hanging joyfully in the wind, cut in two so they would not be phoning very soon. Then he heard the sacred drum of the village sounding. What did that mean? Its use had been condemned by Díaz many years ago, and it had been mute. It all began to take shape in him that they all were strong and clever and cunning. It was the leaders and the followers who made intelligence. He did not have even to yell what they had done when the group of men sitting on their horses saw him approach, his little pony stretched out like a wire. They were on their way before he could shout or turn his sweating pony.

The whole scene had changed when they entered the town. They could hear the powerful drum being beaten and a joyful kind of roar as they tore down the narrow lanes where the people got thicker and thicker, letting them through. Then in the Zócalo they saw a strange sight. The Rurales and the soldiers had been separated by the crowd, the women pushing them and the little boys pricking their horses. When each one was isolated, he was disarmed, and they each one stuck up out of the crowd, ridiculous, like a sore thumb. The commandant was inside the stable with his pants stolen, and the women and boys made a sound like a million sparrows, taunting the soldiers. Crying and laughing and stroking the legs of the men, the women let them through to cut Zapata's thongs. His horse was brought, and amidst their joy he mounted and the whole posse was off, leaving them men with the Rurales' guns pointed at them. They held them until Zapata and his men were safe. The men got them off the horses, rolling and spitting on them, taking their boots. Then they took from them quirts and machetes and clothing that they wanted, and horses, and left them half naked in the square or walking towards Cuernavaca.

Timoteo and Zapata and all of them took the south road and then straight up the pathless sierras to the hills, having often gone there to Cuerrera to sell horses.

When they got over the first sierra, they all began to whoop and sing, still riding away at a gallop.

Chapter 15

Over two months went by and Tepepe did not return. Timoteo went back to Anenecuilco to help his mother plant. All the guerrillas went back to plant their fields, for they would have to have corn. The hacienda was deserted now, and the sugar mill was closed. The people on the hills slowly came down to their own land, and they had so much to plant and so many animals that had been abandoned and so much meadowland for the graze that the village was a changed place. They had their old fiestas and religious ceremonies. Even the priest had fled.

Díaz had said he was forming an army to wipe out Morelos, but the guerrillas had wiped out Huerta. The army of Díaz held only the hill of Cuautla.

Morelos had gathered over nine hundred men with weapons of some kind. Herdsmen, rancheros, and campesinos sprang out of the ground and occupied the mountains, the roads and the fields. Now they did not have to meet the enemy with slingshots, knives and machetes. They had armed and claimed themselves from the haciendas and the trains of Huerta.

The Magnani brothers joined them with a printing press. They came from Philadelphia and knew such history about the United States, and every evening in Tepepe's house they printed leaflets which the young took out in the day and in the night.

Every night Timoteo and his mother watched and waited for Tepepe, and Timoteo went up to the charcoal forests, past the loaded donkeys bringing charcoal to Mexico City, and asked them if they had seen such a man. He knew that under the loads of the donkeys often were hidden rifles and ammunition to be hidden in the forests.

Alfredo had gone to Mexico City.

The villages were different than he had ever seen them. "Do we look like people who have broken out of bondage?" he asked. He found himself quite famous for his journey into the prison of Cuernavaca. "Did Zapata really say that to you?" He had never heard so much talk—had speech also been a prisoner? They were no longer the silent and blind villagers Zapata had described as white rabbits, for now they had speakers. And hidden in their pockets was the paper printed by the Magnani brothers and sent to them. Those who could read taught others who could not. Timoteo himself could teach the alphabet to the village children, making out the letters with a stick in the Zócalo or in the fields. Others passed the border guards, drifted like smoke through the armies of Huerta, and told how the people of Morelos had been robbed of their election and how they were all going to join the forces of Madera in the north. The men put a big thumb on the letters and waited for night to appear at Tepepe's house to have them read.

But Tepepe did not come.

Zapata said a thing could happen to the old shepherd. It took time to come safely through, and nobody knew what was happening between the north and the south. There might be some fighting. Nobody even knew what was happening in Morelos. The soldiers of Díaz marched through along the road at night, but it was through a deserted countryside. When they stopped to camp, they often woke in the morning with the guards tied up and all their guns and ammunition without a trace. Some of the soldiers even deserted and brought information and guns to the army of Morelos. "Even the stones were Zapatatistas," they said.

Everything was changing. Friends they never saw came down from the city. The Magnani brothers started a school. One day, a pretty school teacher, a woman, came also and talked about how they must have school. "This was not an army," she said. "This was a rising people, and they must learn as they fought, learn to read, learn history and counting." She not only talked, but one day a bell in the church rang, and she started a school in the church. At first, only the mischievous little boys came, and she taught them. Then others began to hang around watching, and she drew them in, and, last, the women timidly came. Timoteo's mother was one of the first. She was very brave, sitting down and taking off her rebozo and waiting. Here I am, she seemed to say, waiting to be taught.

He was very proud of her.

And one day, riding up with twenty horsemen all covered with sweat and dust, who had ridden over the mountain from Mexico City, there was Alfredo. Timoteo hardly knew him. He had grown, and he had a little fuzz on his face and carried a rifle like a veteran. "Alfredo!" he cried, and Alfredo turned in his saddle, and Timoteo realized by his look that he also had changed. Then the strange rider cried, "Timoteo!" and jumped out of the saddle. They embraced each other, then shyly looked at each other, and then began to laugh instead of crying.

Everyone ran out of the school and the office in Tepepe's house to hear. They had come from the city where there had been a terrible happening (come for harvest instead of planting).

Díaz had ignored the election of Madera as he always did any opposition. In May, thousands had gathered outside the government palace in Mexico City demanding his recognition and the seating of Madera. They hurled stones through the windows, but Díaz, who had an abscessed tooth, refused even to come out.

Alfredo and Timoteo ran to their hideout on the river. Alfredo, walking up and down in excitement, began to tell him.

"I tell you, mi amigo, you never saw anything like it, nor will again. Díaz was going to have a great celebration for the grits of Dolores Day. It would cost twenty million pesos, banquets, pageants, balls. He had ordered twenty carloads of champagne. It was his eightieth birthday beside. Imagine in the face of starving people to put on this show. It shows they have no sense even to care for themselves. There are rebellions everywhere, Timoteo. You never heard the like. In the north, there is Villa. In Juárez, Madera had slipped into Texas to save his life and come back. Provisional government was formed, and they came into Mexico City. I tell you, Timoteo, you should have been there. Mobs filled the streets, Sonora, Durango, Sinalon, the miners, the Indians, the fishermen, everywhere ready to rise. In front of the palace, we were waiting for his resignation. It was packed solid, one person next to another. Friends surrounded Díaz's bed. Then suddenly, without warning, just as here, the troops began firing from the balconies of the national palace, from the cathedral towers, firing point blank on the crowd.

Some fired back, but hit no target, The crowd could not run. When the plaza emptied, there were the dark dead lying on the pavement, some said two hundred, three hundred—who knows?

"And where is Díaz?"

"Oh, my brother, after midnight Díaz resigned. I tell you there was madness. I joined some boys beating American gasoline drums. What a noise! I tell you, they were running out of there like rats—governors, politicos, cientificos—getting their money together and running out of the country. They'll let him get to Vera Cruz with his gold, and then he will go to Europe and never return, that old man, that terrible old man."

"He is gone?"

"Yes, they let him go."

Timoteo walked around beating his hands together. "So that's the way it happens. Just ran, ran."

"Yes, he is gone."

Both boys began to howl like coyotes and beat each other on the back and laugh. Alfredo began a new song he had learned.

Señoras y señoritas
Those who have not looked upon a field
Where men driven by some wonderful dream
Are willing to die
For something they have never seen
You are looking at them now
The hombres of Zapata.

A crowd soon came around them to learn the new song, and guitar players, and soon they were roaring it out. Then the horsemen went yelling around the Zócalo, and another ballad singer was making up a ballad for that day and occasion. An army seemed to be forming right there. "Let's go to Cuautla and shoot the locks off the prison door. Let's drive to Cuernavaca!" they cried. The tired men who had come over the mountain were tired no more, and they were ready to take the news of Díaz's flight over the countryside. Already the Montana brothers were setting up type in Tepepe's hut to get out leaflets in the mysterious print, and the teacher was helping them. Timoteo was walking around like a lord, his arms around his mother, who was laughing and singing like a young girl. Men ran to the corrals to get their horses.

The women brought the guns. Others would follow on foot. Zapata's brother turned as they left and cried, "Only men with horses and gun now. The rest of you bring in the corn harvest. We will need food now. Get you a gun and horse and join us!"

Timoteo joined Alfredo, who admired his new horse. He embraced his mother, who reached up to give him a bag of tortillas. The men knotted their sarapes so they could not be followed and then took the path over the hills.

The revolution had come.

Chapter 16

They were waiting for the committee to come down from the hills with the plan of Ayala. Tepepe was the center of argument since he had suddenly in the night appeared at his hut in Anenecuilco, looking even better than when he left. He had been put on a train after meeting Madera and delivering his message and had ridden like a prince with food and his horse in the baggage car. He had much to tell, bringing back the message from Madera about how to organize a provisional government, seize their own food from the enemy, drive Huerta out of Morelos, and wipe up the last of the thieves holding out in Cuautla. They laughed at how Madera had instructed them in guerrilla warfare. Never meet a well-equipped army head on, fight at your own time, on your own ground, draw them, harry them, mutilate them, ambush, retreat, lure them then withdraw, fade away, get lost. He tells us as if we haven't been doing that for a thousand years!

"He is a little man, a lawyer," Tepepe said, "but he has the campesinos in mind. He promises us democracy, the vote, without imposition. He does not know the south, but he will learn. Madera is waiting for us to drive Huerta's army out of Cuautla. Well, we will."

They were camped in the mountains under the tree of Ayala. It was to be called later a historical tree.

On the fourth day, there were three thousand men gathered. Deer and goats were roasting on spits over a perpetual fire. Singing and talking went on all night. The boys brought in the cracked bell from the village to ring at the historic moment. There were whole bands ready to play.

But where were Montana and the little Ink Pot and Zapata and the Magnani brothers and the teachers from Mexico City who had brought what was called a little typewriter to write the plan all down?

Have they brought us into the wilderness and left us? They did not come.

All the jefes from the states were there, all dressed in their best and came in strange costumes of the Conquistadores, with Spanish embroideries and elegance. Most kept their own calzones, their white pants and shirt, and what were to become known as the Zapata sombreros, huge and beautiful hats with embroidered ribbons hanging from them. Great stories were told and tears were shed for their own men hanging from trees along the roads of the mountain. They had stopped to cut them down and bury them. As they told their stories, Alfredo and Timoteo sat as men among them, remembering their own deed, the fathers and Anaya, and they listened sometimes modestly, telling their own stories. The big men would laugh tenderly and look at the young boys now made men. The mountains would lean above the sombreros, the faces under them honed by the intense passion of their freedom. Even the rocks seemed to listen to their cry for justice, for freedom.

The sisal workers told how they had read the northern newspaper to the whole countryside, weaving the rope under the eyes of the guards. They had learned about Madera from Juárez, not a humilde like themselves, but a man who could read and who knew the law, and who was throwing his forces in with theirs. The men had a hard time to keep their fingers in the rope as he read that, in the state of Morelos, they were led by a man named Emiliano Zapata. Timoteo listened with pride and astonishment to know that they were known.

How did such information get to Santo Luis, Missouri? It was the magic writing and reading. The Ink Pot maybe wrote it and sent it by horseback to the city, where maybe it went on a train part way and was picked up by another horseback rider or by charros. He didn't know and maybe would never see. Some day he would like to thank them. This writing and reading was a miracle. He did not know what might exist in those books and how could he even tell if the reader was reading it right? He might even be in a book someday, written by someone not born yet who would collect all the memories from all the people and make a story. Montana and the Ink Pot would surely keep a record. Maybe at this moment they were making these strange marks on paper that another could read. This could be sent to a far country where they had some kind of machine that made many copies, worked by men he never knew. He could not think beyond this, and he squatted listening to the reader.

He knew the Ink Pot would write down on this machine, fast as a man could talk. Other people far away would read of what they were saying this night in the dark in the beginning of a great struggle that would not even be begun for nine years and would go on for many before they get their land. Others would know of this.

One man told how he took guns underneath the hay, and another planted his guns in his watermelon patch.

As Eufemio spoke and made them laugh, what a card he was, careless loud talker, good-humored and full of the stories he picked up at bull fights, running horses, gambling. He was a good man to weld people together, and they loved him. He was older than Emiliano, but of a different breed.

The concheros were playing and singing over in the woods.

Then a strange thing came out of their night singing, of their pooling of their strengths, of their brag and their bone. A man said, "This is all one country, the Americas. It is from the North Pole down to Tierra del Fuego." The men were stunned by their own thoughts, something that seemed to rise and come from them, from a little center like Anenecuilco, like a pebble that makes rings outward. "The people we do not know in North America, in 1776 threw a stone when they revolted against their oppressor. Now it rings softly, like the tide rising engulfs us. America of the Indios. No, it will be America of all. What are they? Many kinds as we are, of many kinds."

On the fifth day in October, the scouts rode in. "They are coming!" the guards shouted. The three thousand campesinos rose with their guns and formed a line at attention. Dressed in his finest, Zapata rode at the head, and then Montana, looking more dwarf-like and smiling, and the Ink Pot and the others and some from Anenecuilco rode in with bags of tortillas hanging from their saddle bags.

Timoteo sounded the trumpet, which echoed around the hills. The men from Morelos unfurled a silk flag, their own flag, with eagle and serpent. The carbines were lifted in salute.

The sun shone towards afternoon after the men had eaten. The long table they had rough hewn from trees was filled with the committees and the chief men of the villages and the provisional governments of Guerrerro and Michoacan. Montana gave a speech first as chairman, saying that, if you were going to rule your own land, you must have a plan. Everyone understood, and it was this plan they had been writing for four whole days in the mountains. They pledged themselves, their lives and their sacred honor so this plan is a statement to the world. The men seemed to get a little taller. The bands played then. The Ink Pot shifted the papers he had. Zapata leaped to the table. "I give you a name, amigos. You are the army of the south. From now on, united victory to the last man. The liberator army of the south!"

"Viva, liberator army of the south!"

"It is a very grave time, amigos," Zapata said. "I want you to listen to this plan for which many have given their lives already. It is grave. I will ask you, chieftan by chieftan, to vote for this plan or against it. Any man who does not want to support this plan may depart. We will give him food and passage, and no blame to him. We have seen that justice for the people will never be given us by correctos in top hats. It can only be won by the people themselves. You are those who saw his father's land wrenched away from the hands that tilled it. You are those who have seen the villages where he was born stripped of their milpas. Now you are here to listen to the plan we have drawn which we will listen to under this great tree in the land of our ancestors, the Plan of Ayala. We say here that we take back what is ours. We take back the land."

A tremendous shout went up. "It is all we want, and it is what we fought for over a thousand years. It can be said our revolution was born in Ayala, under el arbol grande in the little valley held in the crest of the Sierra Ayala. I, like you, cannot read because of the stupidity of our conquerors, so Montana will read this too. Our first secret meeting was held here so I have called it the Plan of Ayala. Listen carefully."

Then you could have heard a pin drop. The stocky Montana took the paper from the Ink Pot, and he said, "We are pledging men to their blood. Those who pledge this will step forward and sign when they have heard. You can feel you can go home with honor if you do not agree. We will give you horses and food."

So he read the articles. There were many, and they were numbered, and Timoteo listened carefully. Here was some history, warning that promises of land and liberty had not been carried out when men came to power. Woods and land, it said, had been torn from the communal village by legal tricksters and tyrannical force. These lands, it said, are hereby restored to possession of the rightful owners, and all villagers who have lost their lands are to enter upon them and hold them with arms in hand. It seemed so simple. This applied to the land held in common since the ancient Indian nations. Now the divided and ancestral communal lands of the villages were to be returned, and also the landless were to get land. Those with no claim should get the divided and unclaimed land from the haciendas, which should be seized and divided. Some of this land was to be paid for, and those haciendados who refused were to have their land seized and a third paid to the revolutionary fund for the widows and orphans from the war. Vast numbers of peons without title who were forced off land, out of villages, were to have the divided land so there would be no landless. A third of lands and woods shall be appropriated without indemnity. Absentee landlords should have all lands confiscated.

The last article said that Madera must fulfill the promises they had made to the revolutionists of Morelos.

The ragged army was lost in wonder, hearing it put into words.

Then it further said that, upon the triumph of the revolution, the chieftain or representative of power was to call an election, heal the terrible wound the country had suffered, and elect a first provisional government and then a government of the people by the people and for the people.

When Montana had finished, Zapata leaped on the table again and cried, "Amigos, you have heard the plan, and it is up to you to vote. But even if I fight alone to the day of my death, I will fight to make it a fact. We are not banditos, but honest men fighting for the cause, a people's army with a banner of conscience and a plan. The liberation army of the south. I give you that name to define the Plan of Ayala. I say to you that anyone who signs and gives arrest assent and who then fails us and turns his back on us will become a traitor and will die as such. There will be in the future no mercy in this organization for the man who goes back on his word. We are pledging men to their blood. Those who will pledge this will step forward and sign."

There was a moment of silence, and then they began to come forward and form a line. Timoteo found himself in that line of heroic men. One by one they leaned over, and some wanted the name of their mother or father on the paper, dead or alive. A band began to play. Timoteo proudly signed his name, not even printing it, among the XXX's and marks, and then he ran for his bugle. Someone was ringing the village bell. As the men signed, they gave a whoop and began to dance alone or in rings, and some cried "Viva Zapata" and some cried "Viva Libertad" and some cried "Tierra y Libertad." All the Indios, even the stones, seemed to be shouting.

Chapter 17

"Well," Tepepe said, "we could, two buglers like us, turn a battle ourselves."

Alfredo laughed.

Timoteo said, "Verdad, it's true, two buglers like us can give charge, withdraw."

"Never withdraw." They were all crouching down in the arrays outside Cuautla, where the last battle of Morelos against Huerta was to be fought.

"Why is Madera leaving the drunk Huerta in here if Díaz has fled with all his gold to another country?"

"Zapata will have to ask Madera that."

Alfredo and Timoteo had, for that matter, been organizing an army of the lost boys of Mexico City who had poured into the valley. They had donkey packs where they gathered food from the villagers and brought it to the armies of the plains and, in turn, brought ammunition. Many women and children, including Timoteo's mother, lived in the hills above the villages and came down, crept down, at night to bury the dead and to care for the corn and animals. In the night, Huerta's drunk army would run off the animals, the boys would creep up on the camps, set them loose, and they would all come home.

They could look up the barranca and see the cathedral on the hill above the town where Huerta's soldiers were holed in. "There is no way to get up there," Tepepe said, "but to tunnel under and dynamite below—the hundreds of walls, gardens, little streets would be suicide." Tepepe was a dinamatero. He learned it at Puebla. "That's the way we did Amecameca. The valley opened to the Ajuscos and we had to push Huerta back. When we took the town, I will tell you it was something to see how we set up a provisional government in one day better than any government they had had since the Indians."

It was the afternoon of the third day. Tepepe came back so black you could not recognize him, and he fell beside Timoteo and slept. Before he slept he said, "They are fleeing now to the west. They are trying to get out. There were many dead. You could not count them. Alfredo, also exhausted, said, "Is this the price for human freedom? I didn't know it. Is this the way all these centuries it has been fought over?" Timoteo felt like crying, but he too fell asleep. You could not, sometimes, tell the sleeping from the dead.

The sound of the bugle was the only way to give commands to the rebels scattered, converging the second day upon the garrison. Some had fled, some had deserted and joined the rebels, but the big guns still held in the center. They could not approach the little machine guns without being mowed down with their primitive weapons.

No one had slept since two days previously, when the battle had started. Timoteo had to follow Zapata and the peasant generals who directed the battle and blow the signals. Retreat, advance, hold. In the night of the second day, he felt he had no more wind and no more courage. Even Zapata said, "Are there only young boys fighting this battle? I have seen more young boys than in any nightmare." And he had turned away in anguish. But they were fierce fighters, hurling themselves over the walls, throwing the stones down, coming on one wave after another, crawling over the previous one that had been mowed down. Fierce, they had devised ways of appearing behind the dreadful machine guns, of one by lassoing the gunners, or forcing suicide squads and running head on toward the machines, throwing homemade grenades, bottles filled with dynamite with a fuse. They had put many of them out, and now they could see that another day would do it, if they could stay awake.

Zapata and Timoteo and two grizzled farmers, whose beards had grown, lay behind the wall just to the west of the Zócalo. No one had had any sleep or a bite of food. Neither had Huerta's army. Zapata said, "Sleep is liable to win this battle. I saw a gunner actually fall over dead asleep, and another took his place, unable to wake him."

Timoteo felt like crying, but you did not cry any more. The very old shepherd and the very young sat in the afternoon sun among the dead. Timoteo could think of nothing to say, thinking of all the men they had turned over and looked into their dead faces, trying to remember what was their village, who were their wives and children, whether they had been shoemakers, weavers, shepherds. Suddenly everything seemed to change. He did not know afterwards whether he heard the sound of the bullet. It must of exploded in Tepepe's heart instantly, for he just slumped a little toward Timoteo, and it was as if a live bird had flown up and away, leaving only the place where it had been. His eyes were open but empty as a ledge from which the bird had flown. He was simply gone. Timoteo could hardly move. He could see nothing. "Tepepe!" he called, as if he was simply leaving to join his flock as he so often did. "Tepepe!" But he did not answer. A little trickle of blood came out of the side of his mouth. Timoteo did not move. He felt the heavy body. No one was about, and he didn't care if the sniper got him too. He just sobbed, and from a distance you would have thought an old man leaned against a boy and they were talking.

Timoteo was shaken by Alfredo. The whole besieged town of Cuautla was in a heavy smoke, an acrid smoke. He choked.

Alfredo, who had gone to see what was happening, held his tail of his shirt to his nose. "It is zacata smoke," he choked. "You know how it routs bees. Ignacio Maza, you know, who grows chilies, had it all gathered up and fired." They heard coughing, choking and cries of surrender, yelling, cursing, the thundering of horses as Huerta's men tried to get to Cuernavaca or Mexico City. The chili gave a dense, acrid smoke.

"We'll get the rest out," Alfredo said. "Remember those oil drums by the river that say Standard Oil? Come on. They make a loud sound." They ran through the chili smoke to the river and gathered as many of the hidden boys of their boys' regiment as they saw sleeping or peering out, covering their mouths. They began beating the oil drums, making such a sound that awoke the sleeping, and they saw them tear out of the walls, the caves, and take to the roads running.

The campesinos had been divided in relays to attack the cathedral and hold those prisoners within.

Thirty-six hours they had not slept. Neither had the enemy.

Then Timoteo sounded the bugle—for victory.

Zapata said, "What about them now, verdad, los hombres de sombrero, ancho, calzón blanco y huarache."

"An army of the people," he said, "has arisen. Don't forget the sandle-footed ever. Go home," he said to Alfredo and Timoteo, embracing them. "Go home and sleep, and tomorrow reap the corn that is all yours."

Timoteo cried, "But Tepepe is dead!"

Zapata looked down on the old shepherd. He knelt down and picked up the heavy white head and kissed him.

Timoteo thought he had the face of his father, and he also knelt and took the white head in his arms. "I will bury him in the meadows."

Timoteo could scarcely remember the agreed-upon signals. One for the east to advance, two for the west, three for the south, four for the north, and it was not clear who was there to advance. They had won the battle and did not know it.

The regiments in the town had escaped, running up the river several hours before. The silence was the dead. They did not know either how the town was filled with corpses and the river ran with blood.

They simply looked out at the few stunned gunners who looked out at them and received their fire. This was the sole enemy, but they did not know it. Thousands lay dead within the walls. Half of the inhabitants of the town were dead. The rest had fled, out of ammunition, wounded, or crazed. The three men and Timoteo with his battered bugle did not know any of this. They only knew they could hardly see for the gun smoke, the sleeplessness, the horror of what they had been through.

One of the great bearded men—he seemed to Timoteo like a huge and indestructible bear—aimed his gun through the crack in the adobe. Then one of the gunners fell over like a dummy, and the square seemed to shift into a strange peace. The sun shook its light over the shattered trees and the wrecked buildings, and the dead looked like they were sleeping.

Zapata said, "I think – that – was – the – last – one. I think Cuautla is ours. Sound the victory, Timoteo." And he fell over in sleep. The big bear laid his head on his arms along the wall and slept. The other one just dropped on the ground, and Timoteo raised his bugle. And he never knew if he did sound the victory signal, for he too slept.

The whole town fell, as in a terrible fairy tale, into a terrible and deathly sleep.

The few of the enemy left in terror, picked their way over the dead and the sleeping, unable to tell one from the other, and fled to Cuernavaca, where they told a terrible story, and the army evacuated toward Mexico City.

And Cuautla was tranced in a deep sleep. But the state of Morelos belonged to the people.

Chapter 18

Timoteo and Alfredo stood on the edge of their little milpas and looked down at the ancient town of Anenecuilco, the village of their ancestors. They felt a wonderful quiet. The sounds of clashing metal, of the whip, of the shouts of slave drivers, the bustle of mule packs taking their wealth to far ports, the carriages full of well-dressed Spanish women—all was gone. Instead they could see in the bright sunlight in the Zócalo a group of men and women gathered around and gesticulating, turning to point in every direction with great excitement. The little Ink Pot sat at a table and the teacher from Mexico City sat at the funny instrument known as a little typewriter next to him.

"What is happening?" Alfredo asked.

Timoteo put Inocencio back in his box. "I don't know," he said. "Let us go see."

His mama came up, and she too began to point and sweep her hand around the valley, a woman with land again. "They are all bringing in their memories," she said, "of their own land boundaries and the village communal lands.

"Do you remember, Mama?" Timoteo asked.

She looked at him. "Cu-cu-cu," she laughed. "Do I remember, my little owl, my old owl, my warrior son! Does anyone forget their land, their mother, that gives them the food of life and nourishes their children? If I was dead, I would remember the land of my ancient fathers. If you cut me in little pieces, each piece would be a map of the lands that gave us our squash, our beans, our life."

"You are a general, mama. Whoever has a passion for the land, Zapata says, is already a general!"

"Yea!" she cried. "And it is ours again. The hacienda is still. The machines are ours. We can reap what we have planted. It is ours!"

"It is ours!" both Alfredo and Timoteo cried.

"They are opening the ancient grants and maps," she said, "and the old, the ancients, will point out where boundaries went, where the village lands, and the milpas of our fathers."

"We shall no longer be hungry in our own country," Alfredo said.

"I must hurry," she said, "and go down and point out our fathers' lands."

Timoteo said as they went down the barranca, "It is the land. Land before liberty. There in the prison that night, with Zapata, we said the land was everything. A man with someone else on his land is robbed of his dignity, as well as his food, and robbed of his language, his culture, his all."

Alfredo began to sing, "We are the sons of Morelos. We are the sons of Juárez. We are the sons of Zapata."

Even the corn seemed to thrust its long green stalks into the air and cry, "Zapatistas! Zapatistas!"

Everyone seemed to be descending the hills and coming through the valleys, serious and latent, upon the Zócalo, remembering memories that had been taboo, that they hadn't dared to remember, seeing their land rise up again as some flowering woman released from dungeons.

Mama was embracing her friends and neighbors. The talk was low and intense. Two old men were talking about if they should pay the haciendados for the land, and some said they should and some laughed—pay the thief for what he stole? Pay the man who stole your watch and returned it only at gunpoint and bloodshed? Are we fools? We made much money for them. They live in Paris and own race horses worth more than a village of men and women. They took the wealth of our land and our bodies.

Around the table, the Ink Pot was marking on the map, and the teacher was copying down what was said. There were arguments. Was the land of the village owned by them all? Every man had in his mind the outlines of his past freedom and working of the land. It was on his skin like a tattoo. It was in his body and the memory of his working. There out of a wooden box, spread in the sun, were the famous ancient papers. Franco had carried them during the battles and hidden with them in the woods. There they were, open in the sunshine, in the ancient language of Nahuatl that only one man from Tepotzlan could read. He stood interpreting. The old lands seemed to rise out of the clenched hands of old grandfathers.

Looking at the ancient papers with awe, Timoteo remembered a campesino coming from an ancient village to ask himself of Zapata, "What are you fighting for?" And he showed him these titles to the land, and he said, "These are the records of constancy and uprightness of our people and their relation with the land, as a record of a family. This is what we are fighting for, the family of man, the power of man in titles stronger than death, stronger even than justice."

He saw that some of them turned as they described their land and looked back at the hacienda, the high dark walls, in a kind of dread, as if through those gates could come again the Rurales with those terrible guns. There stood armed there only their own fathers and brothers, guarding the door through which they all seemed to have come as if from some dangerous cave where they had been held in a nightmare as serfs and slaves.

Alfredo and Timoteo stood as near as they could to the yellow papers opened to the sun and to justice. Looking at them, he saw his father's hands and face. All the ancestors appeared as the land seemed to open into the air. There, as if by some magic, the old and young men walked again, pointing out their lands, and the women blooming like flowers, picking up their skirts and running out and pointing, and some running to their land, which they could have kissed. The air and land seemed to open and embrace the people. Yes, that's what it meant, for the people by the people. Juárez took that from Mr. Lincoln and it was true. When the people had their land and their own government, there was justice for all. Rights and roots and everything from the fruit and flesh, the rain and thunder, will be ours, falling on our own need and unfrightened fruit and flesh.

Timoteo could see their own fruit—mangos, bananas—beans, chili, coffee beans, our own cows and calves. Your ancestors, he thought, have woven a cloth of brothers and sisters. They have shown us we can survive together, make our own laws, bring forward ancient strengths.

Timoteo's mother had pushed forward, and the crowd parted to let her pass and put their hands on her shoulders and embraced her. She glowed like the young land and the air. She got to the table and leaned her black head to the Ink Pot and pointed to the ancient map. Then she turned and beckoned Timoteo. He was let through the crowd and nodded his head as her calloused finger pointed out their ancient milpas and their water rights, and it was written down.

So they came all that evening and for days after. The text of the ancient document and the reality became one. What was voted for by the people became law. No soldiers lashed them to work in the fields. No whistles sounded from the mill summoning them to payless work.

That evening Timoteo took Inocencio out. He took long jumps as if he too were free. As they ate, his mamacita said, "Soon we will move down into the village in our old house papa built."

Timoteo felt that his papa and Tepepe came up the darkening path and squatted beside them and held out their hands for a tortilla. Something from the past was in the air. Not a sound of jingling spurs, or the cry of the army billeting down for the night, or the shout of soldiers. Below the village seemed to unloose like a knotted fist. A lullaby seemed to come from the freed furrows of the fields. The animals made soothing noises of sleep, strange low sounds and a silence of sleep, as if rest came after a terrible disaster and loss. The air did not carry the sounds of slavery. The land was theirs at night, too.

Inocencio hopped, catching night moths. Timoteo's mama put her arms around him, drew him close, and sang an old lullaby.

Pajaro cu cu cu, poor little bird cu cu
And poor little owlet cooing too.
Rub rub rub, pat, pat pat
When they feel cold, when they want to eat,
The little chicks go cheep, cheep cheep.
Here comes the mom, eating a tuna
And dipping her spoon in the laguna.
The cross-eyed cat had a beard on her chin
That tickled her fat.
Shall I tell it again?
Pajaro cu cu cu.

Chapter 19

After the crop was in, in November, Alfredo came running up the hill, shouting, "Villa has taken Juárez ! Madera has declared a provisional government. The whole of Mexico is free!"

Timoteo and the whole village ran to the Zócalo or from door to door spreading the news.

There were meetings to discuss Madera's plans. Some did not trust a lawyer. Zapata came and spoke before the newly elected council, urging that they meet with Madera. Runners came with news of how Villa had taken the north with an army of men, women, children, and animals, who rode on the trains from battle to battle.

More news came of the formation of provisional governments. Then Madera entered Mexico City, just a hundred miles away.

The day came when Zapata said that the whole state of Morelos would meet and parade before Madera to show him the strength of the agrarian revolt and demand support for the Plan of Ayala. This would mean everybody would come to Cuernavaca, and they would parade before the new government and see the government themselves and decide if they would support it.

So on a fine fall day near the winter solstice, the parade started from the eastern towns of Cuautla, Jojutla, Amecameca, Yautepec. The women rode carts, some walking or on horseback. It was a holiday.

On the way across Wolfe Canyon, they stopped where Timoteo's father had been killed. There was a little cross to mark the spot. They prayed and told the many dead the land in which they lay belonged again to the people. They blessed all the other dead and the ruined villages.

Timoteo had his bugle carefully wrapped, and his mamacita had baskets of delicious food and had on her white blouse and blue rebozo his father had loved on her. The women wore their brightest rebozos, and the babies were wrapped, nodding and sleeping over their mothers' shoulders. The roads were gay and crowded. The men wore every adornment of silver and sash and sat on their fine horses, and some sang. Timoteo blew greetings and signals when he was asked. When they neared Cuernavaca, Zapata rode out with Montana, his mustaches fiercer than ever. Timoteo sat on his horse and blew the Diana. Everyone roared as they entered the town of Cuernavaca. Timoteo hardly recognized it from the dark town he had entered to go to the prison that night, and the elegant gentlemen and ladies had all fled—where? Back to Spain, to Paris? They had taken what jewels and money they could carry, but they had left the land.

The palaces were empty. Timoteo thought that the palace of Maximilian and Carlotta is empty. The palace of the governor is empty. Why, Zapata would be there. It would be his palace. He would be governor. He had not thought of it before. The people would have to truly elect him. Yes, he surely would be elected.

Everyone was pointing out the great empty mansions and who had left them. Then they all entered the Zócalo, where they saw the army of the people in their great white hats mounted solid around the whole market and Zócalo, guarding them all. They did not trust anyone. They had been betrayed before and would be again. "On guard," Alfredo said. "We are on guard."

The walks and streets were lined with people, in masses, packed solid, cheering the villagers as they came in, running out to meet friends. How they had taken the city, the city of their conquerors. Stories were told—how the governor had fled, how the Rurales couldn't get to Mexico City fast enough, how they ran on foot over the mountains, how they tried to take their wealth with them, but they had no servants to carry anything. How they couldn't carry much themselves. How one man drowned, his pockets weighted with gold. How the road to the city was strewn with what they had dropped.

Timoteo had to leave his mama and go to the stand where the speaking was. He was to join all the other horn blowers and be in the bodyguard of the campesinos of Anenecuilco, the birthplace of Zapata.

Then the people were silent as Madera came in a carriage, with his own guards close to him and the big white-hatted

Morelos army riding before and behind him like a great flock of white birds.

Madera came out of his carriage and mounted the steps to the stand where he greeted Zapata, fierce and bright in his fine embroidered pants and jacket and his huge hat and his mustachios bristling. Below there was dancing and the mariachis played the ballad of the Morelos revolution:

> Señoras y señoritas,
> Those who have not looked
> Upon a field where men
> Driven by some wonderful dream
> Are willing to die
> For something they have never seen.
> They do not know the hombres of Zapata.
> I will tell you of these men
> They are great angels,
> Filthy, hungry angels,
> Full of jokes and love,
> They throw themselves before you in the fight.
> At night they break a tortilla,
> A cigarette with you.
> Señoras y señoritas,
> These men that die,
> They are the soul,
> The soul of Mexico.

Timoteo was watching Madera. He had never seen such a small, little man with such a face and elegant clothes. He did not trust him. He was a lawyer too. But Zapata said if he could unite the country, he was their man.

He looked timid and frightened beside Zapata and Montana.

Then Zapata spoke, and the crowd hushed and were like starving people given food at last, given justice.

He told about how the land had been taken from them. It sounded terrible as he told it. Two families owned all of their nation. The wealth went away. The people lived in poverty.

Then he said how they had fought, raised an army—a people's army—and claimed the land according to their sacred writ. Like a wound, he said, the country's history had opened at Anenecuilco.

These were new words. The people listened as if raising on their shoulders a cathedral of ideas. Sometimes there was a low rumble of assent, then they fell into the silence in which they seemed to bear towards the slight, fiery, tense burning figure of Zapata.

Timoteo stood with his bugle clutched close to his breast, and he couldn't hear it all. Sometimes it was like music, and sometimes he spoke in the Indian language, and then into Spanish and some Anglo words. He was speaking from the blood, as his mama would say.

He told how provisional governments had been formed, no state police, each village governing themselves, no authoritarian or bosses, he said, no dictators, and a low roar went around the tightly pressed crowd and some turned to tell the next row out who could not hear what he had said.

He told of the election of the village jefes, the council meeting to partition the land along the old communal lines, how the stolen land was reclaimed orderly without greed, how agrarian commissions and surveys were made with the water rights for all. He told how in one session they had restored the old economy and, for the first time, there was food for all: corn, chilies, tomatoes, chickpeas, onions and fruits. No high prices. Local production and consumption. No one-crop sugar economy.

"We extended our awareness," he said, "to guerrilla war, and now in communal government which we won ourselves. We do not want to own the land and the fruits at the expense of our brothers and sisters. We want to bring back the rich land of our forefathers, the fat animals, the fruits of many kinds, the product of our land and labor. We know how to live in one place with tradition and happiness."

The words formed a new life in them. They all thought the words came from inside them. It existed in them all—the virtues, the skill, the grace of their fathers.

He then told Madera that they had their Plan of Ayala. They asked only for what was their own and what they had fought for. This plan says what we want and what we will have. "We ask you," he said, "if your government will carry out this plan. You see, we will show you our power. Eight thousand men will parade before you here, armed with the weapons of liberty. If you follow our plan of the land, we will support you."

Timoteo saw that Madera needed them. They did not need Madera.

When Zapata finished, there was a great outcry. Viva Zapata! Viva Zapata! Viva! Viva! Viva!" The sound must have gone to Anenecuilco. Then Timoteo lifted his horn and gave the call for the parade. The far bands began to play and the mariachis all at once, as if the very stones had broken from long silence and the hoofs of conquerors' horses to cry "Liberty!"

From the far side of the plaza, the parade entered the street. The people fell back and made a bright passage for them. The drummers began a din, and all the nations marched together with banners, the splendid riders and the women and children. They all waved and shouted to Zapata, who stood beside Madera, and the long parade went by.

There were village bands and trumpeters and ancient war horns and ancient drums carried to five men and beat upon by two. They all wore a motley array of clothes, some stolen from army officers, French plumes, jeans, and mostly the white calzones of the little rabbits of Zapata, who had shown how to fight a superior armed force. The streets were jammed, and the shouts and vivas were many. There were tall dark men from the mountains, hook-nosed and lean, boney coffee-colored and agile men from the south, and the Guerrero men who had come up for the fighting in white pajama suits and embroidered cartwheel hats. There were squat, powerful older men who had fought the French, a contingent of the dreadful dynamiters, the suicide squads that furnished supplies to the guerrilla army. There were blocks and blocks of the beautiful women of Morelos carrying their babies in their rebozos, many of them barefoot and many who spoke only their mother tongue and had refused the speech of their conquerors. There came the red-sashed girl contingents with their ammunition belts across their breasts like the men carrying their guns who had fought at Cuautla, and a fiery beautiful girl with her braids cut off and her straight black hair forming a crown.

She played a trick which Madera saw only because her hair was cut. She led four blocks of the Amecameca army and the young buglers around the Zócalo, and they appeared three times. In this way, she thought it would make Madera think they had more of an army than they did, but he kept seeing the same bobbed haired and vivid girl, and he spoke to Montana and they laughed heartily. Madera was astonished at the beauty of these people, their faces speaking of remote time.

Timoteo saw Tepepe's lone horse in the ranks of the battle of Cuautla, and Tepepe's bugle hung from the horn and his old rope bag and his quirt and his gun. He and Zapata saluted, and Timoteo felt the hot tears behind his eyes. "What a bloody struggle—the struggle for freedom—and how many men go down who will never have it." Tepepe the shepherd had said and who could not read. Timoteo vowed that he would become a teacher when this war was over. He would teach a whole generation about the fight for freedom. He did not know that they would fight nine years more, six years to the constitutional convention where they would write a great document of freedom to match the one in North America, reflecting all the struggles and intelligence of both the living and the dead. He did not know that Zapata would be assassinated because he refused to be bought or to yield one inch on the Plan of Ayala—all the land now to the people.

On this day, they were flushed with victory. They had moved out of blind darkness to take over their own fates, and proudly they marched in the brilliant sun of fall, and proudly Timoteo waved to his mother and she waved back, and he turned and smiled at Zapata.

Zapata smiled back, and the new flags of their heroic people flew above them—the new flag of the new Mexico.

About Meridel LeSueur

Meridel LeSueur's poetry, short stories, and novels are a beloved part of the cultural and political fabric of our times. She was one of the great women literary and communal voices of the twentieth century, which her long life spanned. Meridel was born on February 22, 1900 in Murray, Iowa, and died in Hudson, Wisconsin on November 14, 1996. Meridel wrote, "I was born at the beginning of the swiftest and bloodiest century at Murray, Iowa in a white square puritan house in the corn belt..." She described her own roots as springing from "preachers, abolitionists, agrarians, radical lawyers on the Lincoln, Illinois, circuit. Dissenters and democrats and radicals through five generations." As a child she lived in Iowa, Kansas, Oklahoma, Texas and Minnesota. She believed in giving voice to people's struggles. She said she learned early to write down what they were saying, hiding behind water troughs in the streets, under tables at home— listening. Listening to the tales of the lives of the people, her writings were grounded in these grassroots, salt-of-the-earth stories and experiences of working people, of the poor, the disenfranchised, the dispossessed. She strove to make history a living, moving entity in our lives. She once said that words should heat you, they should make you rise up out of your chair and move!

As a young woman, she studied physical culture and drama in Chicago and New York City and she plied her talent in the silent movies in California as a stunt woman. As a young activist she lived for a time in Emma Goldman's commune in New York City. Throughout her life she wrote from and was part of the great social and political movements of her time. Her writing encompasses proletarian novels, widely anthologized short stories, partisan reportage, children's books, personal journals, and powerful feminist poetry. Her early works, in addition to profound working class consciousness, are also focused on the struggles of women, and particularly poor women, those sterilized without their consent in so-called mental hospitals, those on the breadlines, those whose lives and oppression more traditional leftwing ideologues did not comprehend. Her children's books found heroes and sheroes in US history, and are especially noteworthy for their non-racist depiction of Native American peoples and cultures. Meridel believed her writing could be a bridge making connections across many different cultures.

Her timeless writing brings us the voice of our grandmother Meridel—a voice of revolutionary wisdom and indomitable resistance. As she said, "survival is a form of resistance." Meridel saw Halley's Comet twice, once when she was 10 years old and again when she was 85—we are certain that the impact of her work will be felt the next time Halley's comes around .... and the next ... and the next .... seven generations and more from today! Meridel's life and writings testify to the profoundly democratic idea that positive social change always bubbles up—and sometimes erupts—from below.

From The Publisher

Meridel LeSueur began working on *Zapata Is Here!* in the late 1950s, during a time when her work was actively suppressed and her voice largely excluded from mainstream publishing. Known for her fierce commitment to telling the stories of working people, Meridel researched and drafted this novel after traveling with her family through Mexico, gathering oral histories and community stories about Emiliano Zapata and the revolutionary struggle for land and dignity. The manuscript remained unpublished, until now.

Zapata Is Here! is being published for the first time by Midwest Villages & Voices, the small press Meridel co-founded with her daughters Rachel Tilsen and Deborah LeSueur in the early 1980s. Since its founding, MV&V has published Meridel's *Rites of Ancient Ripening, Winter Prairie Woman, This with My Last Breath, The Girl*, and supported the film *My People Are My Home* by the Twin Cities Women's Film Collective.

This novel is a window into Meridel's lifelong belief in the power of collective memory and people's movements. The story of Timoteo, his beloved cow Cleofas, and the stirring figure of Zapata speaks to the enduring struggles for land, literacy, and liberation.

This first edition includes a foreword by Meridel's grandson David Tilsen, who as a child traveled with her through Mexico during the novel's research phase. His memories and insight illuminate the personal roots of this extraordinary work.

Meridel once said that after her great-grandchildren were born, she realized her audience was just being born. Today, some of those great-grandchildren and others in the family have formed the Meridel LeSueur Family Circle to join with MV&V in reviving this book and continuing her legacy. *Zapata Is Here!* is part of that new phase of an old dream: to bring the stories of the people to the people.

Midwest Villages & Voices
www.midwestvillages.com

www.ingramcontent.com/pod-product-compliance
Lightning Source LLC
Chambersburg PA
CBHW030630120726
47904CB00006B/2098